BRUTUS

is

CHOSEN

THORA HOINES

Published in Australia by Sid Harta Books & Print Pty Ltd,
ABN: 34632585293
23 Stirling Crescent, Glen Waverley, Victoria 3150 Australia
Telephone: +61 3 9560 9920, Facsimile: +61 3 9545 1742
E-mail: author@sidharta.com.au

First published in Australia 2025
This edition published 2025
Copyright © Thora Hoines 2025
Cover design, typesetting: WorkingType (www.workingtype.com.au)
Bible verses quoted from: Authorised King James Version

ISBN: 978-1-923439-05-4

*This book is written by inspiration of the Holy Spirit
and is a tribute to the Lord Jesus Christ for His Greatness
cannot be measured and Our God and His Father
seeks to Glorify Him to the Highest Place.*

FOREWORD

I recall one Sunday morning when Thora came to the altar for prayer. There was no mention of what her need was, nor did I ask. After praying a generalised prayer, Thora turned to walk back to her seat when the Holy Spirit prompted me to ask her, 'Do you write books?' Thora's countenance lifted as she said yes. The Holy Spirit encouraged her to start writing again.

When the Holy Spirit inspires an author to write as He did with Thora, one finds oneself deeply engaged in the story, making it virtually impossible to put the book down.

I truly admire how Thora manages to capture and incorporate the tapestry of various cultures and blend them into a captivating storyline.

There are many passages I could highlight from this book; however, the one that captivates me the most is Brutus's lifechanging experience when his eyes looked deeply into the eyes of the crucified Christ. How true today – an experience for many who lift their eyes and look unto Jesus, the author and finisher of our faith. A graphic and emotional experience which will grip the heart of every reader.

The message of the love of God flows seamlessly throughout this story: His kindness, forgiveness and acceptance patiently waiting for a response, especially from those who feel they deserve it the least. As with Brutus, when a person finally comes to the end of themselves and surrenders to the amazing grace of God, they find the true meaning and fullness of life.

The effectiveness of Thora's writing introduced me into the personal life of a seemingly fictional character. After reading the book, I was left with the impression I had known Brutus as a close friend. I'm confident your experience will be the same.

It is my prayer that this book be distributed far and wide. We would do well to gift this book to family, children and friends, especially those who have wandered from God or have never known Him.

May God bless you.

Rob Urban
Founder and senior pastor of Logan City
Christian Church
and United World Ministries
Queensland, Australia

Contents

Brutus	1
Dismas	21
Cornelius	29
At the Zebedee home	53
Back to Jerusalem	59
Back at the barracks	73
Home at last	83

BRUTUS

Brutus grew up in Rome, the eldest son of a family with deep roots in the Roman military. Some of his earliest memories were of the pomp and splendour of that great city. He had been raised in a home steeped in military traditions, and as far back as he could remember, he had been fascinated by it all. He loved to watch the grand spectacle of infantrymen all dressed ready for battle with their colours unfurled marching to the beat of drums, and the powerful cavalry horses carrying the grim-faced men who looked so majestic and purposeful. The sight and sounds of the Roman war machine around him caused an adrenaline rush in his strong young body, and he longed for the day when he would be old enough to join men like these – to be respected in society for being part of an elite group and to be held in high esteem, and able to experience the personal power afforded him as part of this great army. He watched the cavalry officers in their striking uniforms and envied them; he vowed that one day he would be a Roman officer, dressed like these men and riding on a big powerful horse. Nothing was going to stop him.

Brutus attained his goal and became a centurion in the Roman army. He was a tall muscular man and looked magnificent in his snow-white tunic. He was an imposing figure and vain enough to enjoy the way the crowd parted as he approached and allowed him to pass. He had served Rome with conviction and dedication from an early age and had proved himself to be a great leader. His men respected and admired him; this gave him a deep sense of pride and satisfaction. The very things that were the daily routine of any fighting man's life had forged a strong bond between him and his men. They were hardened soldiers, tough in mind and body, a close-knit fighting team, and he was proud of them. Together they had faced the countless armies of countries Rome had wanted to conquer in her quest for power and dominance. Brutus could trust these men to obey his every command. They were willing to pay the ultimate price, because the thing uppermost in their minds was to serve Rome.

Brutus and his men were looking forward to spending time with family and friends and renewing old acquaintances. He felt it was time for him to settle down and start his own family. He had been thinking about Diana a lot lately, and he planned to visit her when he returned to Rome. However, his plans would have to wait, for he and his men were being sent to Jerusalem for the Passover season of the Jewish people. This festival had great significance because it commemorated a time in history when the Jewish people had been freed from slavery in Egypt. They passed over the Red Sea on dry land to live in their own homeland once again, the land that God had promised to their forefathers through Abraham, Issac and Jacob. It was easy to understand that, as this event drew near, the people would be preparing for a time of celebration and thanksgiving.

Brutus was feared for his cruelty by those who opposed Rome but respected by the Roman hierarchy for his courage and skill in battle, so Pilate, the governor of Judaea, wanted Brutus to be personally responsible for making sure that Jerusalem would remain calm and peaceful during the festival. People of the Jewish faith would be streaming into Jerusalem from far and wide. Some would stay with family and friends, while others would have to find lodgings close to the temple. There was a feeling of great expectancy and excitement among the Jewish people at the prospect of visiting the great temple, soaking up the atmosphere of this great city, spending precious time with loved ones and renewing old acquaintances. Jerusalem would be teeming with people and the animals they would bring with them to be sacrificed on the temple altar. It would be a time of deep reverence and thanksgiving for the great things God had done for them in the past.

Pilate knew that these people, and especially the temple

hierarchy, despised Rome and all those who upheld its pagan rule. He also knew that among the temple priests there were certain troublemakers who would like nothing better than to take this opportunity to stir up the crowd against Rome. Because he feared a disturbance among the Jews, he had arranged for more military personnel to be on duty than normal. He was determined to keep peace in the city. It could cost him his job if the Jews began rioting in the streets and things got out of control. Rome could no longer afford the expense of housing garrisons of troops in the major cities of her colonies, and it was his job to keep the peace in his region. The Roman way was to use maximum force and brutality to quell any uprising as quickly as possible. Pilate intended to use all means available to him.

Early one morning Pilate was awakened by a member of his staff. He told him that the leading Jewish priests, elders and temple guard had gathered on the pavement near Herod the Great's old palace, which was now used as the Roman Praetorium, and were waiting to see him. They had arrested a man named Jesus of Nazareth, and the Jewish hierarchy wanted Pilate to sentence him to death. He knew they were using him, because under Roman law, they were not permitted to sentence a man to death. These leaders were shrewd and manipulative, and Pilate was uneasy about their demands. He had heard about this man named Jesus and he knew that the Jewish hierarchy hated Him. Jesus had a reputation for being a good teacher and would spend hours teaching the people from the ancient Jewish writings. He told the people that God loved them and wanted to help them, and He would perform miracles to prove His point. He was very popular with the people, and great crowds followed Him everywhere He went; this made the Jewish leaders envious and angry.

With a deep sigh, Pilate made his way to where a crowd had gathered on the pavement. The Jewish leaders would not enter the building as, according to their law, it would defile them, especially as they were about to celebrate the Passover feast. Hidden from view behind some heavy curtains, Pilate observed the crowd, noting that the full strata of society had gathered. Some had that indefinable air of having wealth and influence, obviously loyal to the religious leaders. The poor were there too, thin and unkempt. Pilate knew that they would have been influenced by money from the temple coffers. He groaned inwardly as he observed the assembled cross section of humanity and knew instinctively that the temple hierarchy had been planning this gathering for some time. The next few hours were going to be difficult.

As Pilate moved into view, the crowd turned to face him, all eyes fixed on him. Even before he had time to open the proceedings in the customary manner, the temple hierarchy and some of the people began shouting out accusations against Jesus. Pilate threatened to exclude them from the proceedings unless they voiced their charges against Jesus in a more orderly fashion. Again and again, they brought accusations against Him, as first one voice was heard shouting from the crowd, then another, and still another. Although the accusations against Him were inconsistent, their hatred and hostility towards Him was very evident.

Pilate was angered by their attempt to show themselves as something they were not. He felt the real reason they wanted Jesus dead was because He was so popular with the people and they were not. The whole charade was a gross imposition on his position as governor and on his time. Then from somewhere in the crowd, a voice was heard to shout, obviously angered by the seeming slowness of the proceedings, 'We found this fellow corrupting the nation saying that He himself is Christ the King.'

Pilate turned to Jesus and said, 'Are you the king of the Jews?'

Jesus replied, 'You say that I am.'

Pilate turned to the high priests and said, 'I find no fault in this man.'

The high priests became angry again and accused Jesus, saying, 'He has stirred up the people from Galilee to Jerusalem with His teachings.'

When Pilate heard that Jesus had lived and worked in Galilee, he decided to send Him to Herod, who was the governor of Galilee but was in Jerusalem for the Passover season. He hoped that Herod would take up the responsibility and sentence Jesus. Pilate could find no fault in the man worthy of death, and he did not want to be bothered with the Jews wrangling and petty jealousies. Most of all he wanted these troublesome Jews to leave his domain, as they had already taken up too much of his time. Then he ordered that Jesus be taken to Herod.

Herod was pleased to see Jesus because he had heard about Him and was hoping to see Him perform a miracle. He questioned Him at length, but he too could find no fault in Him worthy of death. This man was the son of a carpenter. What did it matter if He called Himself the Son of God? To his knowledge, this man's name had never been linked to a militant group. On the contrary, His motives seemed to be honourable, and Herod wanted no part in His execution. After the soldiers had mocked Jesus, Herod sent Him back to Pilate. Once again in front of Pilate, the accusations continued, and the religious leaders became more and more aggressive. Pilate was amazed at the calm, dignified composure of the prisoner. He stood quietly, not saying anything in His own defence, but would sometimes answer if asked a direct question. Pilate got the feeling that Jesus did not see Himself as being on trial but rather fulfilling His divine destiny.

During this season it was customary to release a prisoner of the people's choice, so Pilate asked the people, 'Whom will ye that I release unto you? Barabbas or Jesus, who is called Christ?' (Matthew 27:17).

When it appeared that Pilate wanted to release Jesus, the high priests got the people stirred up all over again and they shouted angrily for His death. The crowd was becoming louder and more hostile with each passing moment, and Pilate felt fear mingled with panic take hold of him, as he realised that he could lose control of the proceedings. The tensions seemed to be reaching breaking point; one thing he could not allow was a riot in the streets. He was also afraid that Herod, who was partly responsible for governing the region with him, would get to hear of the commotion and think that he could not control the situation. Pilate was well aware that the Jewish leaders were powerful enough to play him off against Herod to get what they wanted. To them, Jesus was a radical who opposed their ethos; and they hated Him and wanted Him dead.

In the midst of all this turmoil, Pilate's wife sent him a message saying, 'Have thou nothing to do with this righteous man, for I had suffered many things in a dream because of Him' (Matthew 27:19).

After reading the note, Pilate wanted more than ever to set Jesus free, but the Jewish leaders became frantic. They were desperate to get rid of this man whom they hated. They objected to the fact that when He addressed the crowds, He gave himself many titles, and the one they hated the most was 'Son of God'. This made Him equal with God, and according to their reasoning, this was blasphemy. He had performed many miracles and knew the scriptures better than they did, but they still would not accept Him. They shouted with even more hysteria than before, 'Crucify him, crucify him, and let His blood be upon us and our children'. What a shocking statement to make! They were prepared to curse themselves and their children to get what they wanted.

With that ringing in his ears, Pilate turned to the guards who were standing near him and gave the command: 'Bring me a bowl of water and a towel.' Anxious to keep the peace, he washed his hands in symbolic fashion. While drying them, he said, 'I am innocent of the blood of this righteous man; you see to it.' Then he gave the order for Jesus to be flogged and crucified.

Brutus called out an entire regiment to the courtyard of the Praetorium to mock and humiliate the prisoner. Scourging and crucifying a man did not bother him or his men; they were true men of war and unmoved by human suffering. Brutus had been given orders and, true to his character and training, he carried them out beyond the call of duty. The soldiers removed Jesus's garments and began to perpetrate the most horrific mutilation of any human being in all of human history. It has been faithfully recorded that He was marred more than any man and beyond all recognition.

After Jesus had been flogged and the soldiers got tired of taunting and humiliating him, Brutus gave orders that He and the other two men to be crucified should be taken to Golgotha. He had selected three men for the task. They were strong and knew the routine. Their job was to nail each man to his cross and then raise the heavy cross up and place it into a deep hole in the ground. They were seldom able to perform this strenuous manoeuvre without difficulty. The aim was to get the upright section of the cross partway over the gaping hole, then raise the cross up so that it would slide down into the hole. Being heavy and cumbersome, the cross would come to an abrupt halt as it reached the bottom of the hole, causing shock waves of agony to surge through the man's body.

Jesus had been calm and dignified in Pilate's presence, and afterwards in the courtyard, He had displayed that same dignity. Now, as Brutus and his three men nailed Him to the cross, He cried out in pain, but He spoke no words, nor did He struggle to free Himself. The soldiers were aware of the sharp contrast between Jesus and the other men whom they had crucified. It was commonplace for a panic-stricken prisoner to fight the Roman soldiers with every fibre of their being, and it often took four soldiers to subdue their prisoner. They would have to tie him to his cross with ropes before they could drive the nails into his hands and feet. Then, as he hung there writhing in agony, he would scream curses on them and their families. The four men agreed Jesus was the complete opposite of any man they had ever crucified.

After the execution, the soldiers decided to share Jesus's clothes out among themselves and cast lots for His seamless robe. The deep wounds made to Jesus's body by the cat-o'-nine-tails had bled profusely and the beautiful robe was soaked in blood. Jesus watched from the cross as the soldiers gathered up His clothes. His heart ached with sorrow and love as He thought of the precious people who had given Him the robe. He knew how costly it was, but He also knew that they loved Him and wanted Him to have the best robe money could buy. He was sad to see how bloodstained and dirty it was, and because the soldiers treated it as merely a prize to be gambled for. They did not realise His emotional attachment to it, nor to the people who had given it to Him. But these people would understand His decision to wear the robe on this day. They knew that He always gave His best, and today was no different. He would give His best to the soldier who had led the team to crucify him.

The place where they had laid the heavy cross on His back was clearly visible; it had pressed deeply into His wounded flesh. The soldiers could see at a glance that, despite the bloodstains, the dirt and grime, each piece of His clothing was the very best quality. Apart from His twelve disciples, there were certain ladies who were part of His inner circle, like Mary Magdalene and Joanna, the wife of Chuza, who was the steward of King Herod Antipas, ruler of Galilee, and many others. Some of these ladies were very wealthy, and because He had healed them and helped them, they wanted to help Him in return and were happy to provide for His needs from their private funds (Luke 8:2–3).

Brutus and the three soldiers handled each item of clothing, not questioning their right to do so, and ignored the fact that the clothes rightfully belonged to Jesus's next of kin. They simply enjoyed their position of power. Although Brutus was tempted to take the beautiful robe for himself, his men meant a lot to him and he loved them like brothers. Putting rank aside, he went along with their decision to cast lots for the seamless robe. This way, they would all have an equal opportunity to possess the prized garment; it was the least he could do. The four men spread out the clothes on the grass, then they rolled the dice and gambled for them. Brutus rolled the winning numbers. It was a beautiful garment, no doubt about that, and he was pleased that he had won it in a fair game of chance and not acquired it because of his senior rank. The three men watched as he picked the robe up and were pleased that he had won it. They could tell from the way he handled it that he had wanted it all along. Marcus was delighted to have Jesus's tunic, Lucius chose the sandals and Stephanas wanted the money belt. They were all pleased with their newly acquired items of clothing, and Brutus would arrange for the robe to be cleaned. By the time he got it back, it would be restored to its former glory. He would enjoy wearing this costly garment; these seamless robes were renowned for their softness, comfort and beauty, and were made from the finest wool. As Brutus handled the garment and felt its soft texture, something stirred deep within him, something he could not define. It seemed to touch his very soul, and he felt saddened that they had taken the man's clothing in a final act of disrespect.

Later, as he and his men sat guarding the prisoners,

Brutus looked up at the man named Jesus on the middle cross. Their eyes met and held, and Brutus was aware of that strange, deep stirring within himself again. He knew that the eyes of a man express what is in his soul and, as their eyes met, Brutus realised that there was no trace of any hatred or condemnation in Jesus's eyes; instead, they conveyed a message of forgiveness. He glanced in the direction of his men to see if they too were aware of what was taking place, but they were sitting and keeping watch on the prisoners and the crowd. Brutus returned his gaze to Jesus's face, feeling the need to confirm what he thought he had just seen in His eyes. As he searched His face and looked deeply into His eyes once more, sure enough, there it was again. This time, Jesus's eyes seemed to convey a deep message that tugged at his heart, yet he had no words to describe what he felt.

Casting his mind back over all that they had done to this man, the realisation that Jesus felt this way was startling and confusing. This was the first time Brutus had ever felt any regret for carrying out orders. Could he trust his own senses, he wondered. He had lived by the sword for many years, and he owed his life to his senses and instincts. Something very strange was happening here. How could any man forgive those who had treated him with so much cruelty?

Brutus had just experienced something he had never known before and realised for the first time just how cruel and callous Rome could be. He thought of the pomp and splendour, and the way the ruling class indulged themselves, giving no thought for the basic needs or the well-being of the common people. But this man on the middle cross cared deeply for all who came to Him. Deep within his soul, Brutus was touched by the sight of Jesus in agony. His whole body was wet with blood and, as Brutus watched, it flowed freely from His many wounds. His hair was blood soaked and caked to His head from the angry thorns that had been woven into a crown and placed on His head. The blood ran down His body and dripped from His feet onto the cross and finally made a pool on the ground. As Jesus hung there gasping for air, His body growing increasingly weak from fatigue and loss of blood, Brutus was saddened by what he saw, and he regretted the part he had played in the whole affair. He felt ashamed of himself as he remembered that he had begun the punishment by striking Jesus full in the face with all his strength. The action was like a signal to all the soldiers, who immediately began to assault Him.

Once more, their eyes met and held, then Jesus turned His eyes to heaven and said out loud, 'Father, forgive them, for they know not what they do' (Luke 23:34). This prayer, uttered from a dying man's lips, was incomprehensible to Brutus. It was the last thing he had expected to hear.

Their cruelty was not justifiable; after all, there was no record of His ever harming anyone.

Everyone knew that all the charges laid against Him by the scribes and Pharisees were fabricated and malicious, simply because they were unpopular with the people, and for good reason. This man was very popular because He had helped countless people. His popularity was evident by the large crowds that followed Him everywhere He went, just to hear Him speak, and to see Him perform miracles. There were things about this man that Brutus didn't fully understand, and as he sat there on the grassy slope, he began to scrutinise the crowd that had gathered to witness the execution. There were those who stood around in groups and mocked Him, saying, 'He saved others; Himself, He cannot save.' But there was also a group of men and women standing near the foot of the cross who appeared to be close friends and family of the teacher, for their shock and distress was very evident.

As Brutus sat there watching this group, somehow it took him back to the day he had been in Capernaum and had first encountered this man named Jesus. He still had a clear recollection of the large crowd gathered in the streets of the city. Some had come from as far away as Tyre and Sidon, some had come from Jerusalem and others from many other towns and villages along the way. They had all come to Capernaum because the Rabbi Jesus was there, and they wanted to hear Him teach. They had never known a rabbi who cared for them, or who showed so much compassion. The crowd discussed this man at length, and Brutus realised that this was no ordinary man. They said He taught in the synagogue with authority, and even the religious leaders could not match His style or His knowledge of the Torah. The people were talking loudly and excitedly as they made their way to the hillside just outside the city, where He was said to be teaching.

Brutus had decided to join them. He was wearing a simple brown tunic that day and no one would suspect that he was a Roman centurion. He stayed a pace or two behind the group walking in front of him, listening to every word they said, till he got near the crowds on the hillside. Then he made his way forward and found a comfortable spot close to where the teacher was sitting so that he would have a clear view of everything that happened, and he would be able to hear everything that was said. He knew that his superiors would welcome firsthand information about any aspiring new leader of the people. And this man certainly had the charisma and ability to attract a crowd and make a deep impression on people.

Jesus taught about 'My Father's Kingdom', saying things like, 'Blessed are the poor for yours is the kingdom of heaven'. Comments about a kingdom got Brutus's attention, and he looked around at the faces of the people sitting near him. Their eyes were fixed on the teacher's face, taking in every word he said. The teacher began to speak again, and at this point the teacher looked straight at him and their eyes met. For a long moment, they held their gaze, and Brutus felt a connection to this strong man with very different ideas from his own. Then the teacher looked away to address the crowd.

'Unto him that would smite thee on the one cheek, offer him the other also, and he that taketh away thy cloak, forbid him not to take thy coat also. Blessed are you who hunger now for you will be satisfied. Blessed are you who weep now for you will laugh. Blessed are you when men hate you, when they exclude you and insult you, and reject your name as evil because of the son of man. Rejoice in that day and leap for joy, because great is your reward in heaven. For that is how their fathers treated the prophets' (Matthew 5:39-40) and (Luke 6:21-23).

This man advocated peace, not insurrection as he had supposed, and talked a lot about life after death, as though people should prepare their hearts and minds now for an afterlife that was in every way very different from the here and now. To turn the other cheek was a strange new concept for Brutus; he had never encountered anything like this before.

Brutus noticed how kind and patient Jesus was with the people. He didn't seem to mind if they came up to Him and reached out to Him in a personal way, and He was not in any hurry to leave them and go on His way. He was a natural born leader and gave of His innermost self to these people. There seemed to be no end to His selflessness; no wonder the people were drawn to Him, and they would always remember that His eyes were kind when He looked at them.

Just then Brutus heard a gasp go up from the crowd and noticed a small group of people walking towards Jesus. It looked like two men holding a third man between them, who looked as if he was bent over and had no control over his legs. The man in the middle looked dirty and unkempt and was wearing a long dark robe. The scene reminded Brutus of when slaves would unpack cargo from merchant ships and carry shapeless bundles ashore and deposit them in the warehouses. The two men put the man down on the grass in front of Jesus, whose immediate response was one of concern. The crippled man was well known on the streets of Capernaum, as he would sit in a prominent position on the streets of that city and call out for alms. It was said that his family would take him to the city in the morning and pick him up again in the evening; and his job was to play on people's emotions during the day, especially visitors to the city, and take money home to help with the family budget.

This may have been the family's plan, but as they conversed, it became clear to Jesus that the man desperately wanted to be made whole. He was tired of the deception, the constant pain and of being dirty and unkempt. He was also tired of being used by his family, who did not care about him as a person, and the gross discomfort and the lack of dignity he suffered every day. All they were interested in was the money he brought home each evening. He, on the other hand, wanted a respectable life, and maybe one day even a family of his own. But for all that to happen, he needed to have a healed, strong body.

Jesus spoke the simple words: 'Be healed, strength come.'

In that instant, the man stood upright, his body healed.

When the crowd saw this miracle, they erupted in cheering and clapping to show their approval. The man jumped up and down, shouting with all his might, 'I am healed, I am healed. Look, look! I can walk, I can walk.' He walked up and down on his now straight legs. What a time of celebration for the whole crowd.

Those too far from the teacher to see and hear everything that had happened asked the question, 'What happened, what happened?' The message spread through the crowd as people told others about the miracle. As Brutus thought about the man who had been healed, he could vaguely remember him begging on the streets near the synagogue.

Brutus was dumbfounded by what he had just seen. He would never have believed it if he had not seen it for himself. For a long time afterwards, his mind kept going back over the events of that afternoon on the hillside, replaying those memorable moments over and over.

Brutus's thoughts were interrupted by the noise of the people around him, and it brought him back to the present. He was determined to make sure none of the condemned men's friends or relatives interfered with their bodies in any way, for they were his responsibility. Brutus and his men sat there watching the three men on their crosses. It had been a long shift for all of them. The trial had lasted all night and then they had crucified the three men. It was now mid-morning, with no sign of a relief guard to watch the prisoners.

Then to Brutus's surprise, his long-time friend Cornelius came striding through the crowd. He looked very distinguished in his full commanders regalia. He looked athletic and purposeful and the picture of health.

Several years had passed since their last meeting. 'I heard that you were in Jerusalem, and that I would find you here,' he said, as they embraced warmly. 'It's been a long time, too long.'

Brutus remembered the camaraderie that had always existed between them and the banter that flowed effortlessly when they were together. He remembered how Cornelius loved to sit and sip red wine from a silver goblet and tell stories of the bravery and courage of the Roman legions, determined men of war, fighting fierce battles. The pride in his voice had been unmistakable as he told of the strategies and tactics they had used to gain the advantage over their enemies and gain new territory for Caesar. He told of the glorious victory parades on their return to Rome and how ships would be sent to the new colony with governors and military personnel to administer the new territory. It was clear that Cornelius loved his country, its ways, its many contrasts and its people.

'You must come to my home in Capernaum, and spend some time with us,' he said.

'I would like that,' said Brutus. 'It will be like old times. I have much to discuss with you, and much has happened since we last saw each other.'

DISMAS

On the day Jesus was crucified, two thieves were also crucified. The soldiers put Jesus in the middle, with one thief on His left and the other on His right side. Dismas was one of those thieves.

He had been hiding out in the pretty little fishing village of Bethsaida, close to where the Jordan River flows into the sea of Galilee. It was the perfect spot for him to keep a low profile, because he knew that the Roman soldiers were looking for him, and he hoped they would not think of looking for him in such a remote place. He was a wanted man, a notorious criminal who worked with a gang of thieves that had a long history of robbery and violence. He was cunning and calculating, with a very clever brain. But instead of using it for good, he used it to scheme and plot for his own gain and did not care about the ruin he brought into the lives of others. The Roman punishment for his crimes was death. They simply got rid of the unwanted elements in society, and he knew that they would not give him a lighter sentence, because they would want to make an example of him.

One clear sunny morning, after Dismas had bathed in the local stream and was sitting on the bank enjoying the warmth of the sun and the early morning peace and stillness, he found his thoughts turn to the thing that delighted his senses the most. With excited butterflies in his stomach and thoughts that craved fulfilment, he could not resist thinking about possibilities for the next robbery. Should he work alone, or should he contact the others? Their last robbery had been very successful, and there was no real need to contact the other gang members just yet. But while still deep in thought, the sound of human voices interrupted his thinking and brought him back to the present. He moved so that he would be hidden from view, but he did not need to be concerned because they were moving away from him and heading in the direction of the lake. He watched them for a moment and wondered why so many people were up and about so early in the morning, and all heading in the same direction. What did they know that he did not know? So, being a curious man who lived by his wits, he decided to follow them. A crowd always got his attention because he knew it would give him easy pickings and endless opportunities.

Taking the necessary precautions, Dismas pulled the hood of his tunic down to cover half his face and followed the crowd. He listened intently to their chatter and soon learned that the crowd was going to the water's edge, the place where people came ashore from boats. There they hoped to find a man named Jesus, who they knew travelled the length and breadth of the country, going to towns and villages, teaching the people about His Father's kingdom. Wherever He went, He healed all who were sick. It did not matter what ailed them: the lame, the deaf, the blind, the cripples, even the lepers called out to Him for healing. He was always compassionate and easy to approach, always ready to help anyone in need, and the people were overjoyed to learn that He was coming to their village. In their village, there were many people who needed His help. Family members and friends brought their loved ones, not only for His help, but also to hear His stories and His teachings. He was a strong man who gave them hope for the future and helped them forget the repressive society they lived in for a while.

The news had reached them that He was coming to their area. Herod Antipas had just beheaded His cousin, John the Baptist, and He wanted to get away from the crowds for a while and have some time alone with His disciples. But as He stepped ashore, He noticed the crowd that had gathered to meet Him, and when they saw Him, they called out greetings and He greeted them back. Then they all followed Him as He made His way out into the wilderness. They did not seem to mind that the area was quite remote. It was quite obvious they were going to follow Him wherever He went, because with no medical facilities available to them, they were desperate for

His help. After He had been walking for a while, He realised that the crowd that was following Him was growing in number by the minute. Initially, people from Bethsaida had come out to meet Him at the water's edge, but soon the people from the other side of the lake, who had seen Jesus and His disciples leaving in the boat, began to arrive. They had followed them on foot along the shore, and as they went through the towns and villages along the way, the news spread, and the crowd grew larger and larger. Now as He turned to face the crowd, His heart went out to these people who were in such desperate need, that they would go to any lengths to see Him. He noticed their shabby clothes and knew that if they could not work to support themselves, they would soon become destitute, because the family and friends who had brought them could not help them indefinitely. As was the case with any crowd, these people had many needs, and only He could do something about it. Despite their pain and problems, they had followed Him to this remote place. So, although He needed time for Himself, when He saw their desperation, He had compassion for them and began to teach the people, as was His custom, and heal the sick and infirm.

They could tell by the way He looked at them that He wanted to bring comfort into their lives. By the time He had finished talking to them and healing all who needed His help, it was late in the day. The disciples wanted Him to send the people away to nearby farms and villages so they could find food and lodgings for the night. But Jesus said, 'No, you feed them or they will faint on the way.'

'How in the world are we going to do that?' they asked, 'there is not enough money in the bag to feed so many people.'

Then the disciples came to Jesus and told Him that the only food they could find in the whole crowd was five loaves of bread and two fish that belonged to a young man. 'Bring them to me,' He, said, and when the food was brought to Him, He told his disciples to make the people sit down on the grass in groups of fifty. He took the loaves and fish and, looking up to heaven, blessed them and gave each disciple some to give out to the people.

Dismas had been in the crowd and seen Jesus perform miracles of healing all around him. He knew that the lives of these people would never be the same again. They had followed Him out of desperation but would go home with a spring in their step and a new lease on life. He had never encountered a man like this before and could only imagine how healing these people would affect them and all those who knew them. No wonder He was so well known and popular with the crowds. As Dismas sat on the grass with the others, he was given some bread and fish and, as he ate it, one mouthful at a time, there seemed to be no less in his hands, and he was able to continue eating, until he could not eat any more.

Everyone was grateful for the food. What a day it had been! Some of the people in Dismas's group had been healed and were explaining to the others just how difficult their lives had been, and how different things were going to be now that they were healed. No wonder Jesus was known to so many people, and His fame made a place for Him everywhere He went. After they had all eaten as much as they could, the disciples were sent to collect up all the scraps and leftover food in baskets.

Dismas asked the disciple who came to their group, 'How many people do you think are here today?'

'I'm not sure, but judging by the number of groups, at least five thousand men, and some of them have brought their wives and children' (Matthew 14:15-21).

There was a buzz of excited chatter as people all around him were sharing stories about their healings. Then a whisper came through the crowd that the disciples had gathered up twelve baskets of leftover scraps. 'What a miracle,' said someone. 'The whole day has been just one miracle after another. To think He started out with just five loaves and two fish, fed all these people and there are still twelve baskets of scraps left over. I shall never forget this day.'

By this time, it was late in the afternoon and Jesus decided it was time to send the people home. He had worked hard all day and felt the need to rest and have time alone with His Father in prayer. Dismas felt a little envious of the disciples because they had such close contact with this amazing man who had the power to do anything He wanted to do and could meet every need. The day had made a deep impression on him, and he fell asleep still in awe of this man. In the days and weeks that followed, he often thought about the many miracles of healing he had witnessed and the feeding of that great crowd. Every time he thought about it, he marvelled again and again at the great power Jesus had, and that he was in control of every situation, as He went about His mission on earth.

In the fullness of time, Dismas was caught red-handed by the Roman soldiers. They had laid a trap for him and he had fallen into it. This time, his greed had got the better of his good judgement, and now the dreaded day for his execution had arrived. He found himself on a cross next to the man named Jesus, whom he had last seen in the wilderness. He had a vivid recollection of the way He had fed all those people so miraculously and healed all those sick people. He could not understand how this good man had fallen foul of the Romans. He listened in amazement as the people walking past and even the soldiers reviled him.

Where were all the crowds of people He had helped, he wondered. Then, when the thief on the other cross reviled Him as well, Dismas could not keep silent any longer and said to him, 'Do you not fear God, seeing you are in the same condemnation? And indeed, justly; for we receive the due reward for our deeds. But this man has done nothing amiss' (Luke 23:40–42).

Then Dismas spoke to Jesus. 'Lord, remember me when you come into your kingdom.'

Jesus replied, 'Verily I say unto thee, today thou shalt be with me in paradise' (Luke 23:42–43).

CORNELIUS

A few days after the crucifixion, Brutus made plans to go to Capernaum and visit his friend Cornelius. He wanted to see him as soon as possible because he had no idea when they would be sent back to Rome, and there were several things regarding his future that he wanted to discuss in confidence with someone he could trust.

It was customary for soldiers of his rank to be allotted land on which they could farm and raise a family of their own when they retired from the military. The other thing to consider was that his parents would want him to become involved in the running of the family estate. To start from scratch on his own property would be very hard work, and it would take years before he would see the fruits of his labour. The family estate had ample accommodation, and the land was already very productive. His father had many servants and slaves working for him and this made life a whole lot easier. As he thought about these things, he felt that the latter was by far the better choice. Surely Diana would prefer living on the family estate and be able to enjoy all that it had to offer, rather than starting a new project with all the hardships and setbacks that they would have to face.

Brutus respected Cornelius's practical, in-depth approach to problems and valued his wisdom. He also wanted to talk about the latest crucifixion and how it had affected him deeply. He was haunted by those seemingly all-knowing dark eyes that had held his gaze, and the scenes of that day seemed to linger in his memory.

When Brutus arrived at Cornelius's home, he was greeted at the door by a servant girl who said, 'My mistress is in the garden. Come, I will take you to her.'

As Brutus stepped through the doorway of Cornelius's home, it was like walking back through the pages of history, and he stopped for a moment to observe the beautifully appointed room. Oil lamps spaced evenly on the walls lit this internal room full of treasures. Along the back wall of the room was an array of the most magnificent white marble statues he had ever seen. They were all family members from a bygone era. Then there were statues of more prominent public figures that were placed tastefully throughout the room. The servant girl smiled as she waited patiently for Brutus to take in his surroundings. His reaction to this room was quite common with visitors to the house.

Then Brutus's gaze shifted to his left as a splash of colour caught his eye, and there on the opposite wall was a row of ornate gold hooks. Draped over each hook were beautiful cloaks, all made from the finest and most costly fabric in an array of royal colours. There was rich crimson and purples; all the cloaks were trimmed with the most exquisite gold braid. Then among the coloured cloaks, he noticed one that was pure white and trimmed with an ermine collar. The pelts had been cut and joined so cleverly that the collar was a luxurious white with thin black stripes along the bottom edge. It was indeed a magnificent garment. The striking colours of these beautiful garments would have made the wearer stand out in any crowd. Some of the cloaks were long and would have trailed on the floor as Cornelius walked along. They were folded in such a way that the costly gold brooch used to fasten the cloak at the neck was clearly visible. Then there were others that were shorter and would have been worn on less ceremonial occasions.

Immediately above the cloaks was a collection of helmets shaped and designed for the wearer's individual needs and preference. They were mounted on round wooden posts seated in metal brackets fastened to the wall. They would have been worn by Cornelius's ancestors, all officers in the Roman army. The sight of these magnificent helmets gleaming in the lamp light stirred something in Brutus's blood, and he could feel the adrenalin begin to mount in his veins till it almost took his breath away. He could sense the deep pride and power these men must have felt as the helmet was put in place. The plume of horsehair dyed red on top of the helmets would have made them look taller and more fearsome; the intention was to strike terror into the hearts of the enemy. The visor and cheek plates completed the armour. Placed beneath and to the right of each helmet was the warrior's chosen weapons of war. Some had favoured the javelin and sword, while others had favoured the javelin, the sword and the dagger. These items portrayed fierce battles fought and won and were commonplace to Brutus.

Looking at the weapons of war hanging on the wall triggered a flood of memories and, for a moment, it was as if he were right there on the battlefield with his men, the sights and sounds of battle all around him. Vivid memories flooded his mind, and he relived the scenes of hand-to-hand combat: the beat of the drums, the commanding officers' battle cry, the sound of steel clashing against steel, the heat of the day, the sweat, the flies, the inevitable sight of blood, the cries of brave men in agony and death and the involuntary shout of triumph at the death of a doggedly tenacious opponent. Then again and again, the battle cry urging the men on to even greater exploits, was all so familiar. The Roman army was greatly feared and known to win battles even when outnumbered ten to one. These soldiers were like fighting machines; they just went on and on until commanded to stop.

Brutus was intrigued by the styles and colours, and could

not remember when, if ever, he had seen such an amazing array of memorabilia. He could sense the pride and nostalgia with which these items had been displayed at the very entrance to the home.

What a spectacle of pomp and power, thought Brutus, *and so typical of Rome.* There was no mistaking the fact that Cornelius came from a very powerful family, who were steeped in political and military traditions and were accustomed to a privileged lifestyle. But Brutus knew that he was a humble man at heart, despite his great wealth.

As they continued through the house, Brutus was very aware of his surroundings. This family's wealth was very evident. The house was decorated to the highest standard. In one of the rooms, there was a beautiful mural, and in others the floors were covered with Persian rugs, the colours blending perfectly with the rest of the décor. These would have been commissioned, or skilfully chosen, from the shopkeepers at the camel train traders' resting place. Brutus had been at an oasis on one occasion when the camel train from Persia had arrived, and had witnessed firsthand the bargaining between a prospective buyer and the camel train overseer. It had been comical to watch the animated gesticulating as each party tried to get the best price.

The atmosphere was enhanced by a faint fragrance of spikenard that permeated this beautiful home. The Roman upper class, with their servants and slaves, epitomised a euphoric way of life. As they entered the garden, Martha rose from her seat and came towards Brutus, and with arms outstretched, she greeted him warmly.

'We have missed you,' she said. 'It must surely be several years since we have seen you, but you do look well. So many of the old group have been commissioned overseas that we don't see many of the old faces any more. That's why it's so good to see you, and Cornelius will be pleased that you have come to see us. He often talks about you and wishes all these wars were over so we could all live a normal, peaceful life. He is out at the moment but will be home soon.'

With that, she clapped her hands and told the slave who appeared to bring a bowl of warm water and a towel to wash Brutus's feet.

'I must go and attend to the meal,' she said, 'but sit here in the garden. It is cool and pleasant, and I will arrange for a tray of refreshments to be brought out to you. We have another guest coming for dinner tonight. You may know Him. His name is Jesus of Nazareth.'

Brutus stared at Martha with disbelief. Jesus here? How in the world could that be true? For a moment, he felt shock and confusion well up within him, his mind racing with thoughts and questions. He knew that this man was dead. He and his soldiers had put Him to death themselves, and Marcus had even pierced His side with a spear just to make sure. How could He possibly be here now and in person? It was impossible! After what seemed like an eternity, he finally answered Martha, who was perplexed at the lengthy pause in the conversation. Brutus replied simply, 'Yes, I know the man.'

Martha went indoors and left Brutus to enjoy the peace and seclusion of the garden, with its bright colours, sweet-scented blooms and shady trees. As he sat in the shade of a large tree and took in the scene, dry leaves tumbled along the path in front of him, swept along by a light breeze. *How pleasant*, he thought. *No wonder I would like to have a home of my own and live in peaceful surroundings.* Then quite suddenly he realised that was what he wanted more than anything else: a home of his own and a wife to share it with him.

Brutus was as comfortable in the home of Cornelius as he was in his own home, and as he sat there enjoying his surroundings and the solace the garden offered, he suddenly became aware that there was someone else in the garden with him. Whoever it was, was watching him. He could feel their eyes on the back of his head, and it made him feel a little uneasy. He looked around to see who it could be. To his astonishment, standing in the shade of the garden wall and partly hidden by some shrubs was Jesus, who didn't move but rather waited patiently for Brutus to come to terms with the fact that He was alive and was here in the garden with him. Brutus stared at Him in disbelief and could not think of anything to say. Jesus was one of the reasons he had come to see Cornelius, and here He was, standing just a short distance away.

After Brutus had finally regained his composure, Jesus

emerged from His shady spot and walked towards him. His eyes were clear and shining with a zest for life, and His arms outstretched in a welcoming gesture. The scars from the nails were clearly visible on His hands and feet. There was no mistaking this was the man they had crucified. Yet the expression on His face showed no trace of recrimination or malice but rather showed compassion, just as Brutus had experienced on the day of the crucifixion, when He had called out, 'Father, forgive them, for they know not what they do.' Brutus felt humbled in the presence of this courageous man who displayed such strength of character.

Then Jesus placed one hand on Brutus's shoulder, saying, 'I wanted to talk to you because I know that you have been troubled about my crucifixion, and the part you played in it. But I want you to know that everything is all right and that you have nothing to be troubled about. You see, I came to earth on a mission. I was sent here by my Father. As you know, I talked a lot about Him and His kingdom when I was teaching the people, and I have accomplished everything He sent me to do. I left my home in heaven and came to earth. I put aside my divine body, my position of power as God's son, and all that I had ever known living in heaven with my Father and the angels and came to earth for man's sake. I came with one purpose in mind, and that was to redeem man so that he could be in a right relationship with us again. I put on a human body with blood in my veins and became subject to the very ones I had created, so that I could die as a human being and shed my blood to pay the sacrificial price for man's redemption. When your soldier put his spear in my side and the last drop of blood and water flowed from my body, I literally gave everything I had to give. I lived my whole life knowing the horrific way it would end, and I did all this because only my blood can cleanse mankind of every sin that they have ever committed. Only my blood as the Son of God could do that. No other sacrifice would be holy or costly enough to buy mankind back from the devil, and now that my task has been completed, I am ready to return home to be with my Father again.'

At that moment, Martha came out of the house followed by a servant carrying a tray of food for the guests. Behind them at a respectful distance walked two slaves, each carrying a large copper bowl of hot water and a snow-white towel to wash the feet of Jesus and Brutus. The water was comforting after their journey and they both enjoyed the relaxing comfort of the foot bath, but too soon the water lost its heat and became lukewarm. When Martha noticed that the slaves were drying the feet of her guests, she turned to Jesus and said, 'There is someone I would like you to meet.' She called out, 'Tobias!'

A man appeared in the doorway. He was tall, with a muscular physique and dark hair. He walked towards the guests and had a pair of new sandals in each hand. He walked up to Jesus first and, kneeling before him, fitted His feet into a pair of new sandals, then he turned and fitted the other pair of sandals on for Brutus. That done, he picked up their soiled sandals and said, 'Let me take your sandals and I will have them cleaned for you.'

Martha could not contain herself any longer. She stretched out her hand to include Tobias in the conversation, and looking at Jesus, she said, 'I would like you to meet Tobias, our servant. Do you remember the day Cornelius came to see you about him? He was paralysed and in great pain and we feared for his life. He is Cornelius's right-hand man and the overseer who runs our home and all the staff so efficiently that we cannot be without him. He is a trusted member of our household, and we would never be able to find anyone as capable to take his place. That is why Cornelius went out looking for help and saw you in the street with your disciples and a small group of people. We had heard about you from the old man, Zebedee, who owns fishing boats. We have known that family for many years and buy all our fish from them. Since his sons, James and John, became your disciples, Zebedee talks about you all the time. Whenever we see him, he always has a story to tell about the miracles that you have performed, so as you can imagine, Cornelius was delighted to see you that day of all days, talking to a group of people in the street.'

'Yes,' said Jesus, 'I remember that day very well, and I have tremendous respect for Cornelius. He approached me and asked me to heal you, Tobias. I was quite prepared to come here to see you, but Cornelius was adamant that I should only speak a word, and you would be healed. I can still remember his words to me. He said, "I am not worthy that you should come under my roof, for I am a man with authority and if I tell a man to go, he will go, and if I tell someone to come to me, they will come to me and do whatever I tell them to do." I had never seen such faith in anyone before. Tobias, I am pleased to be able to meet you in person.'

Tobias bowed his head respectfully. Placing his right arm across his chest, he said to Jesus, 'I owe you a great debt, master, and someday I will repay you for your great kindness towards me.'

He bowed reverently once more and walked indoors carrying the soiled sandals, then Martha began to serve her guests food from the platter that had been brought out for them.

Just then a messenger arrived with a letter for Martha, and after reading the letter, she said to the two men, 'Cornelius will not be returning home tonight, as he has been detained in Tiberias on an urgent business matter. But I want you both to stay here tonight and get to know each other. As a matter of fact, you may stay as long as you like.'

After the evening meal, Martha led the two men to a comfortable room where the servants had lit a fire. They sank into the deep plush cushioned chairs, and were grateful for the opportunity to enjoy a relaxing evening in front of a warm fire.

'I have asked Tobias to bring you some light refreshment and make sure that you have everything you need,' said

Martha, 'so make yourselves at home, and I will see you both in the morning.'

After Martha left the room, the two men sat staring at the flames in silence for a long time. Somehow, it was comforting to watch the flames as they flickered among the cedar logs arranged in the grate. Much had happened in the last few days, but those events were behind them now, and there were no feelings of animosity or revenge between them. They both just needed some time to be comfortable and quiet. It was Brutus who broke the silence, as though he needed to unburden himself and could not remain silent any longer. Jesus listened as he spoke from his heart and tried to explain his feelings.

'I know you are who you claim to be,' he said. 'The one they call John the Baptist referred to you as the Lamb of God who takes away the sins of the world. On another occasion, he called you the Son of God. This bold claim stuck in my mind, and over time I came to accept it because of several things that happened, and somehow it seemed possible. I was here in Capernaum and heard you teaching on the hillside, and I saw firsthand the miracle of the crippled man being healed. I thought about what happened that afternoon a lot, and then I began to hear stories about you from fellow officers and friends. The things I heard from my colleagues confirmed what I already felt about you. Everything pointed to the fact that you were indeed very different and could well be who you claimed to be, God's Son, come to show men a better way of living their lives. I remember the stories I heard about you. One day, you were teaching at the synagogue here in Capernaum. Then at sunset, some of the people went home and returned with their relatives and friends who had all kinds of sicknesses and diseases. You simply laid your hands on the sick and they were all healed. And some of the people they brought to you were possessed by powerful demon spirits. You simply spoke to the demons, and they left the people.

'I can tell you, nobody had ever seen anything like that before, but for you, it was the most normal and natural thing to do. That evening when the demons came out of those people, they were heard to shout, "Thou art Christ, the Son of God." Even the demons knew who you were and said as much. Most people are afraid of demons, but these demons were afraid of you, and what you might do to them' (Luke 4:40–41).

'I think Pilate could see through the false accusations, and that was why he was reluctant to sentence you to death. He knew you were not militant and tried everything he could to set you free. He even released that scoundrel Barabbas, but the Jewish leaders would not relent. They even accused you of treason because they knew Pilate could not ignore a claim like that, and he was duty bound to do something about it. Nobody else could have borne the torture that happened to you. After you had been flogged, an entire regiment of strong men was called out to assault you. Not only that, but they spat on you and put a crown of thorns on your head, and beat you with sticks, mocked and ridiculed you. The torture just went on and on. I was there. I saw it all. I even had some of your blood on my tunic. In all my years of service to Rome, I have never seen anybody so mutilated and still alive. When they got tired of it all, you were taken out and crucified. No other man I have ever known had to endure such torture. I marvelled as I watched the events unfolding before me, because you seemed to have been strengthened supernaturally to be able to withstand all the verbal mocking and ridicule, and all the physical torture. It was above and beyond the norm. For some reason I can't explain, I felt sure that you were on a mission, and no matter what happened, you intended to accomplish your goal.

'Then on the way to Golgotha, I know you tried to carry your cross, but we could see that you were just not able to. That was why we made Simon from Cyrene come and help you. It must have been about mid-morning when you were crucified, and at midday, I remember vividly the panic I felt when suddenly a great darkness covered the whole land, and it lasted till mid-afternoon. It was like an eclipse of the sun. We were all terrified, not knowing what to do. Nothing like this had ever happened before. We were bewildered but we knew that we had to light torches and be extra vigilant to make sure that nobody tampered with the bodies. But as you can imagine, we were not prepared for this sudden darkness and did not have the means available to light torches, but eventually after much toing and froing we managed to solve the problem. I can tell you, Jesus, that when you called out to your Father and said, "Father, forgive them, for they know not what they do", we could not have been more terrified. The very atmosphere was charged with a strange power that made my skin tingle and my hair stand on end, and there was an eerie silence, as if time stood still and was waiting for something spectacular to happen. Then you seemed to will your own death and wanted to die, so you did. I remember you simply bowed your head and gave up your spirit. My soldiers and I had never experienced anything like that before. Most people fought death till they could not fight anymore. But you did not fight death. I remember, even Pilate was surprised to hear that you were dead so soon after the crucifixion, and shortly after that, there was an almighty earthquake. People moved about in panic, not knowing which way to run, and the noise it made was deafening. It even split the rocks open. I can tell you, Jesus, when all this was taking place, we were so terrified that we were shaking from head to foot, but we dared not leave our post as your guard. It would have cost us our lives. With all that had happened previously, and all that was taking place at that moment, I knew that you were who you claimed to be. That's why I said, "This indeed is the Son of God." You had to be. It was as though the very heavens were getting involved with what was happening on the earth. You even raised people from the dead, like the time you brought the widow's son back to life. You knew that the poor woman would have been destitute, with no one to take care of her in her old age. The temple hierarchy knew they could not do anything like that, and they could see that God was with you. I remember when I had to go and tell Pilate that the stone sealing your tomb had been rolled away, and your body was missing. He had a strange expression on his face, and he just looked at me, waiting for me to continue, and as I did, it was replaced by a whimsical smile. Then he simply dismissed me. I was completely astounded with his reaction. I had expected something, anything, but not that. Then I remembered the sign he had placed on your cross. It read, "Jesus of Nazareth, the King of the Jews" (John 19:19). I don't know if he did that just to annoy the Jews, but he made a point of having it written in Greek, Latin and Hebrew so it would be clear to everyone. Pilate is nobody's fool, and the matter was never brought up again. I also think he trusted me because we have a favourable relationship, and although the guard had changed during those three days, I was back on duty when it happened.'

Brutus seemed to have said all that was on his mind. His voice trailed away, and he became silent. The room was quiet, except for the soft crackle of the burning logs, and because the fire was beginning to die down, Jesus leaned forward and added some more logs to the grate. The room was warm and comfortable, and the two men, despite their vast differences, were enjoying each other's company. They both felt the need to have a frank discussion about their thoughts and feelings, and the events that had taken place in Jerusalem just a few days before. It seemed as though these two vastly different men were destined to be strangely connected by a strong bond of friendship.

Now it was Jesus's turn to stare at the burning logs but not see them. It was as though he were gathering His thoughts. There was so much to explain to Brutus. After a while He began to speak.

'You and your soldiers didn't crucify me, Brutus, nor did the Jewish temple authorities. What you were all involved in and unaware of was that my death and resurrection was the way my Father and I had planned for the redemption and salvation of all people everywhere. My Father and I love mankind more than you could possibly imagine. In fact, we wanted a family so badly, whom we could love and who would love us in return, that we created mankind to be the object of that love. We love you despite your faults and wrongdoings. Our love is not based on your works or good deeds but is perfect and unconditional. Our heart's desire has always been that everyone would be in a right relationship with us once more. When Adam and Eve disobeyed my Father's command to not eat the fruit on the tree of the knowledge of good and evil, they allowed Satan and sin into the perfect world that we had created for mankind, and they did not realise the terrible far-reaching consequences of their actions.

Genesis 2:16 The Lord God COMMANDED the man saying, of every tree of the garden thou mayest freely eat. (17) But of the tree of the knowledge of good and evil thou shalt NOT eat of it: for in the day that thou eatest thereof thou shalt surely die.

'Everything that happened the day I was crucified was a pure act of our love for all mankind. Heaven is a holy place and because it is holy, no sin is allowed in there. My Father is holy and that makes Him just, and a just judge. This aspect of His nature demands consequence for all the sin in the hearts and lives of people, and all that sin had to be dealt with, so that mankind could be in a right relationship with us again. The cruel things done to people and the devastating effects it has on them grieves my Father's heart. Each and every person is very valuable and important to Him. He cares about the weak and those who are easily intimidated and become downtrodden, because they can't help themselves. He also cares deeply when people are cheated out of what is rightfully theirs by greedy self-seeking liars and thieves. When all mankind stands before a Holy God who is a just judge, they will all be found guilty, because they have all said and done things that they know are wrong. And because He is a just judge, there is retribution and a price to pay for sin and wrongdoing. All the collective evil and wickedness perpetrated on the earth since Adam and Eve had to be dealt with. And because mankind in his brokenness was not able or worthy to come before a Holy God and do anything about it, I did what man could not do to make things right again between God and man. As the Son of God and the Son of Man, I bore in my own body the judgement for the sin of all mankind for the past, the present and all future generations. Then when I was crucified, every sin ever committed was laid on me. I paid the price man could not pay. I gave my sinless life to pay the price for the redemption and salvation of all mankind.

'When children are conceived, it is by the father of that union. By the same token, I was conceived of the Holy Spirit in a virgin's womb. My blood was not tainted with the sin found in mortal man, that had come down from generation to generation since Adam and Eve. In this way, God raised up the perfect candidate to deal with the sin of all mankind. As the sinless Son of God, I bore the punishment for their sin. I was the scapegoat and God put the sin of all people on me.

'Because we gave people a free will, and it is not our will that any person should perish in hell, we took on the responsibility to help mankind. If they should make the wrong choice and allow sin into the perfect world we had created, only I could pay the price for that sin. Mankind in his broken state could not redeem himself. That is why I came to earth to undo all the mistakes people have made and bring them up out of the mess they are in. My whole life has been one of caring for and helping hurting people.

'Because of our great love for all humanity, I died for you, Brutus, and I died for the whole human race. I paid a very high price for the sins of all people everywhere. I took your place. The punishment for all sin was placed on me. In fact, my coming was more than that. It was also to make a blood covenant between my Father God and the human race represented by me, the sinless Lamb of God. To enter into this covenant, we are not asking you to do anything except believe and accept what I have already done for you and receive our free offer of salvation and redemption by faith.'

Brutus had been staring at the fire with his chin resting on folded hands all the time Jesus had been speaking, but now he sat back in his chair and said, 'You were whipped and tortured beyond recognition by the soldiers, and after all that you were crucified, and it has disturbed me more than I can say.'

'That's right, Brutus, and because of what I endured, my Father has made things easy for man and has promised to forgive all sin, no matter how bad. My suffering was far worse. All people have to do is realise that they are sinners needing a saviour, and when they come to the Father in my name and repent of their sins, He will forgive everyone who repents.'

1 John 1:9 If we confess our sins He is faithful and just to forgive us our sins and to cleanse us from ALL unrighteousness.

These few words speak volumes; God says that He will cleanse away 'all unrighteousness'. That means it will be as though all wrongdoing never happened, and man will be clean on the inside once more. Not only that, but He will also change their 'want to' so that they will 'not want to' live according to their old ways anymore, but instead they will 'want to' do what is right in His sight, so that God and man can have a harmonious relationship.

Jeremiah 31:33 I will put my law in their inward parts and write it in their hearts; and will be their God, and they will be my people.

'My great act of love and sacrifice,' said Jesus, 'is worthy of gratitude, and all my Father wants is that people should love Him in return.'

The light in the room was beginning to fade and the oil in the lamps showed signs of running out. It was time to put fresh logs on the fire. Realising the late hour, Brutus rose to his feet.

'I think it's time to go to bed,' he said. 'All of a sudden, I feel very tired. It's been a very eventful day, and, as always, your words have great meaning. You have given me much to think about. It has been good to spend time with you, and I shall not forget what we have discussed.'

The next morning, Brutus found Martha and Tobias in the garden. He overheard Tobias saying, 'He must have just disappeared because His bed has not been slept in, and all the doors are still securely locked.'

'I am so glad He came,' said Brutus, 'because I had the opportunity to talk to Him and let Him know how bad I felt about my involvement in His crucifixion. He was kind enough to explain things to me and let me know that I am forgiven. It was such a relief to talk to Him and listen to Him explain the plan of God for all mankind. He is a remarkable man. He came to share His heart with us and then, without any further ado, He simply disappeared. I don't feel bad about the past anymore. He has taken care of all that too.'

The servants had cleared away the ashes from the night before and had stacked new logs ready for the day. When Cornelius arrived home around midday, he found Martha and Brutus enjoying the warmth of a log fire and still discussing Jesus and the events of the day before. As he joined them, they told him all the news from the previous day.

'I tried to get back for dinner last night, but it was just not possible. But then if I had been here, you would not have had the opportunity to spend the evening with Him, and I think He wanted to talk to you.'

'It was a good evening,' said Brutus. 'I enjoyed our time together. He is a remarkable man, and I felt completely comfortable and at ease with Him. For some reason I can't explain, I am drawn to this man. As soon as I can, I am going to make contact with some of His followers.'

'He is a fine fellow who does many good things,' said Cornelius, 'but I am not fully persuaded to follow His teachings. However, I can arrange for you to meet some of His disciples. When you are ready, I will give Tobias a note, and you can accompany him to the house of Zebedee. There he can buy fish for the household, and my note will take care of the rest. But come, enough of this Jesus. What of you, my friend? We have much to talk about, much to discuss. Let us eat now.'

As they walked through to the dining room, he clapped his hands and servants began to serve the evening meal.

Over dinner Brutus was finally able to discuss his plans of retirement and marriage with Cornelius, who agreed with him and added, 'You are not getting any younger, and you need to be established in your life and financial affairs after your military career as soon as possible.' Brutus went to bed that night feeling settled about the past and his future.

At the Zebedee home

One morning after the crucifixion, some of the disciples were at the home of James and John, the Zebedee brothers. Peter was there with Thomas and Nathanael and some of the others. They were all very excited because they had just seen Jesus on the beach, and He had made breakfast for them. It had been so good to see Him again, and they had enjoyed a breakfast of bread and fish together.

The disciples were telling the family how, when they went fishing the night before, they had not caught any fish, but very early that morning, when it was still not light enough to see clearly and their boat was in shallow water, they spotted a man standing on the beach.

'He called out to us and said, "Have you caught any fish?" We thought it was someone who wanted to buy some fish from us, and we had to tell him that we had not caught any.

The next thing He said took us completely by surprise. He said, "Throw your net out on the right side of the boat, and you will catch some." We had worked all night and caught nothing, and now we were in shallow water. But when we did what He said, to our surprise we caught one hundred and fifty-three large fish!" John was the first one to realise something strange had happened, and he turned to Peter and said, "This is a miracle; how could we possibly catch so many large fish in such shallow water? In all the years I have been a fisherman, I have never seen or heard of anything like this happening before. It must be the Lord."

'When I heard that,' said Peter, 'I didn't care about the fish anymore. My first reaction was to jump overboard and go to Jesus. The fact that I had denied knowing Him three times weighed heavily on my conscience. I had gone over the evening of the trial before Pilate a hundred times or more in my mind, and each time around I felt worse about it than the time before. I could not get the memory of that evening out of my mind, and the fact that I had denied ever knowing Him, not once but three times, on the worst night of His life. And then just as He had predicted, suddenly above all the noise and clamour, I heard the clear sound of a rooster crowing in the distance. It was as if all the noise around me suddenly stopped and the only sound I could hear was that rooster. It was at that moment that Jesus turned and looked at me, and I just had to get out of there, so I left and went out to be on my own and have some time with my own thoughts and feelings.

'I will be forever grateful that my precious Lord singled me out for special mention, when in some of the first words He spoke to Mary in the garden outside the tomb were, "Go and tell my disciples and Peter that I am risen." My heart melted when I heard that Jesus had mentioned my name. I marvelled at the grace that emanated from Him, and the willingness to forgive without hesitation so that we could be reconciled. I could not, and did not even want to, imagine what He suffered during those dark hours. Yet He reached out to me, and I knew that He had never condemned me for my actions but rather understood and loved me regardless.'

While they were all talking, there was a knock at the door. Could this be Jesus? They all jumped up and hurried to the door, but when Peter opened the door, there stood Tobias and a little to his left was Brutus. They recognised him as the officer in charge of the crucifixion, and the sight of him sent chills down their spines. What did this mean? Had he come to arrest them all? But why was he not wearing his uniform, and where were the soldiers? They stared at him in silent dread.

It was Brutus who broke the silence. 'Tobias has a note from Cornelius for the master of this house.'

'Hello, Tobias,' said Zebedee, 'has your master sent you?'

'Yes,' Tobias said and held out the note from Cornelius.

Zebedee, still at the back of the group, read it out loud:

I have sent my manservant Tobias, the one you know,

to buy fish for my household. He has with him one named Brutus, a longstanding friend of mine, whom I can recommend. He is of noble character. He has spent some time with the one named Jesus and has told me that he wants to meet some of His followers. I am sending him to you because I know you can help him.

'Come, come, Brutus, you must dine with us today,' said Zebedee and as he spoke, the group of disciples in the doorway parted so Brutus could pass between them. Brutus and Zebedee exchanged greetings, and he was welcomed into their home. They all made their way to the room made ready for the midday meal, and the servants prepared fish for Tobias to take back for Cornelius and his household.

When they were all seated at the table, the ladies of the house brought food and wine for the men. Zebedee turned to Brutus and said, 'Cornelius says you have spent time with Jesus. Tell us plainly all about what happened.'

'I had the most memorable time of my life with your master,' said Brutus. 'I was at the house of my friend, Cornelius, whom you know, a Roman officer here in Capernaum, whose servant Jesus healed.'

'Yes,' said Peter, 'I remember that day.'

Brutus began to tell the disciples gathered around him about the time he had spent with Jesus, starting from when they had first met each other in the garden until they had both gone to bed, not leaving out a single detail, and how in the morning, it was as though He had simply disappeared, because He was nowhere to be found, His bed had not been slept in and the doors were securely locked.

The group of believers were dumbstruck by Brutus's story, and it was a long time before anyone spoke. Each man sat busy with his own thoughts, not even aware that a deep silence had fallen upon the room. Brutus felt as if he were alone in the crowded room, but he knew that he was welcome here in the midst of these men, all followers of the man he had come to admire. The afternoon sun was streaming in through the windows, and he found himself sitting in a shaft of sunlight, enjoying the warmth of the sun as he began to eat his neglected meal.

BACK TO JERUSALEM

The time had come for Brutus to return to Jerusalem and resume his responsibilities. He rose early, intending to depart at first light. The early morning rays of sunlight were just evident and shed a soft light on the landscape. The gentle breeze was crisp and refreshing. Saying goodbye to his two special friends was difficult but he had no choice and, mounting his horse, he set the big gelding at an even pace. The days spent with Martha and Cornelius had been stimulating and thought-provoking; much had happened during his stay in Capernaum and he had much to think about. He had never imagined when he left Jerusalem that he would come face to face with, and spend intimate time with, the very man uppermost in his thoughts. He was glad it would take him many hours in the saddle to reach his destination, as it would give him time to think before he got back into the hurly-burly of army life.

As the hours passed and he got closer to Jerusalem, the more determined he became to go through with his plans. His term of office was almost complete, and instead of extending his service further, he would terminate his military career. It was a good time, as he had just returned from a series of successful overseas military operations and had helped to build the Roman Empire in no small way. If he left at the end of this term, he would leave knowing that he had served his country well, and the Senate would be pleased with the newly acquired territory. In time, it would help to generate wealth for the empire and yield the much needed metals for the ever-growing war machine, and he would be known for his distinguished achievements.

As the afternoon shadows lengthened, Brutus decided it was time to rest for the day. He was weary and he knew that Adamas would enjoy a rub down and a good feed, so he decided that he would stop for the night at the next inn he came to. It was not long before he spotted a small inn on the side of the road. After talking to the innkeeper and arranging his overnight stay, he went to check on the inn's stable and found it to be quite adequate. The young man responsible for grooming the horses was a cheerful, friendly lad, and Brutus felt comfortable leaving Adamas in his care.

The next morning, Brutus rose early. He felt the need to have this tedious trip behind him. As he entered the stables, Adamas acknowledged him with pleasure and was ready to continue their journey home. Refreshed after a time of rest and some simple but good food, Brutus felt that he would like to get to know Jesus better. He could still recall the effect He had had on him, like nothing he had ever experienced before, and something he could not describe. He knew he would like to experience this man's presence and personality again. He knew that the easiest way to spend time with Jesus was to make contact with His disciples again. He would find them in the crowd making their way to the synagogue at the appointed prayer time on the Jewish Sabbath. So that is what he would do. He would wait near the temple on the Sabbath and look out for Peter in the crowd. He had met some of the others but had felt a special connection to Peter. He seemed to be the main spokesman for the group and Brutus knew instinctively that he would be the person to contact.

But on the Sabbath, it was Peter who saw Brutus first and crossed the road to greet him. The two exchanged greetings warmly to the astonishment of onlookers. A simple fisherman and a Roman centurion – this, was something they had never witnessed before. A lowly Jewish fisherman would have been rebuffed sharply for stepping in front of a Roman centurion, but here they were engaged in a friendly conversation. No wonder the crowd stared in surprise.

'We enjoyed your company at James and John's home,' said Peter, 'and envied you because you had spent so much time with our precious Lord, while His meetings with us had all been quite brief. We would like to invite you to join us at the home of Joseph of Arimathea. He is having open house at his country estate. It will be held on the day after the Sabbath, and we would like you to come along as our guest. You will be able to meet a lot of the brethren and hear firsthand what Jesus has done in the lives of so many people.'

Brutus accepted gladly. There was nothing he would like better than to spend time with the followers of the man he had come to respect and admire, and there was always the possibility that Jesus might appear, and he wanted to be there if he did.

On the day after the Sabbath, they all met at the crossroads as arranged. Brutus had decided it would be best to take Adamas so that he could get back to barracks quickly if he needed to. He would lead him on the rein to walk alongside them. The happy crowd made space for the big horse as they all made their way to Joseph of Arimathea's house. As they approached Joseph's home, even before they reached the large entrance gates, they could hear the sound of music and the hum of human voices with intermittent outbursts of laughter. As they passed through the gates and came into full view of the house, they could see that a large crowd had gathered on the lawn in front of the house. Some were seated at tables, and some were relaxing in groups sitting cross-legged on the lawn, while others stood around in groups chatting.

Peter called out to one of the servants who was standing close by to take care of Adamas. The man was happy to be of service and took the reins to lead him away. With Adamas in safe hands, Peter, together with Brutus and the others, walked towards the crowd, looking for a free table. Above the din, Peter heard John call his name and turned to find some of the other disciples had arrived early and were keeping a table for them all.

'What a relief,' said Peter, 'to be able to sit down and rest after that long walk.'

They had arrived just in time, for it was not long until delicious-looking food was brought to each table. Piled high on large platters, the roast chicken, roast lamb, roasted vegetables, bread and cheese, fruit and nuts looked very appetising, and no one could resist such a feast. Not much was said as people ate the delicious food with hearty appetites. As the food on the platters diminished and people had eaten all they could, they began to look around to see if they could see friends or recognise acquaintances with the intention of sharing stories. Brutus stood up so he could get a better view and scrutinised the sea of faces around him, hoping to find Jesus, but he could not see him in the crowd. His calculating mind began to take in the number of people who were there. He soon realised that there must be more than five hundred people present.

Just then Mary, the mother of Jesus, came and sat down at their table. It was obvious they were very well acquainted, and the disciples teased her gently as if she were their own mother. Her eyes were shining and her facial expression was relaxed, kind and caring, as always. 'He is risen,' she said, and could not hide her joy. 'My precious son is risen and all is well. I would love you all to visit me whenever you can, and remember you are always welcome in our home. I will have a pot of barley broth ready when you come.' The open invitation was welcomed by the disciples because Mary's barley broth, with fresh hot bread and butter, was a meal they had come to know and love.

As the afternoon wore on, some of the disciples drifted away to talk to other people, and people came to take their place at the table. Brutus found himself sitting next to a very attractive young lady in her late twenties, and a young man of a similar age came and sat down opposite him. Brutus could not help noticing their fresh, healthy, suntanned appearance, and bright, clear eyes shining with laughter and good health.

'My name is Rachel,' said the young lady.

'And mine is Thomas,' said the young man, 'but what is yours?'

'My name is Brutus.'

'I was once a leper,' said Rachel.

'And so was I,' said Thomas.

Brutus stared at them incredulously. There was certainly no trace of the dreaded disease on either of them now; they both looked the picture of health.

'The day Jesus came into my world was the greatest day of my life,' said Thomas. 'Having to call out "unclean, unclean" all the time made me feel like a worthless outcast. But the worst part of it all was that everyone rejected me and didn't want to be anywhere near me. To be rejected is the cruellest thing anyone can endure. But now, to be able to sit here and enjoy a lovely meal and be accepted by everyone is the most exhilarating experience. I can't express in words what Jesus did for me, or the difference my healing has made to my life.'

'That's right,' said Rachel. 'He is the kindest person anyone could ever meet. My mother and I live in a small stone cottage on the edge of a village. About three years ago, my father died, and because my mother is crippled in her legs, I became the one to provide for the two of us. One day when I was gleaning in the barley fields after the reapers had finished for the day, an elderly man working alongside me began to talk to me. I thought it a bit strange because I did not know him. But I was not alarmed because there were plenty of people around and I just thought he must be a lonely old man, so I listened as he rambled on and on. But after a while, he began to tell me about a teacher named Jesus, who had taught the people from the ancient writings and the prophets of our people on the hillside near His home. He paused in the story for a moment and seemed to be wondering if he should continue to tell me the rest, of the things he had seen and heard. Then he seemed to throw caution to the wind, and it was as if he were consumed by a desire to tell someone about all the miracles he had witnessed, even if I did not believe him. "Never in all my years have I ever seen anything like what happened next," he said, "because once He had finished teaching the people, He would heal all who were sick and lame among those who had gathered to hear Him speak. He even cast out demons." The man was clearly very impressed by what he had seen and heard. I can still remember his enthusiasm. Then one day the priests told me that I had leprosy, and it made me determined to go and see the teacher for myself if He ever came to our village.

'Living in the leper colony caused immense problems for my mother and me, and because I was no longer able to work and provide for the two of us, my mother had to rely on family members, friends, neighbours and any funds the Sanhedrin would give us. Trying to get food to me was a nightmare, and most of the time, I would have to make my way home and eat the food my mother left for me at the gate. On other occasions, there was no money for food so we would have to go hungry. Then one day, some friends and I were sitting in the shade of a large tree and heard what sounded like human voices in the distance. We wondered what was happening. Why were the people so excited? As we waited, the noise seemed to be getting louder, then still louder. Suddenly we realised that the noise was actually getting closer, and just a short distance away, we could see people streaming past on the road, all heading up the hill. Someone shouted out, "What's happening, what's happening?" Back came the reply, "He is here, He is here." "Who is here?" the lepers shouted back. "Jesus is here," came the reply. The word spread quickly through the leper colony. "Jesus is here; He is the one who heals the sick." I knew I had to go to Him, because this must be the same Jesus the man in the barley field had told me about.

'Keeping my distance from the other villagers, I made my way up the hill and stood some distance from the crowd. The teacher talked about His Father's kingdom, where everyone was equal and nobody got sick. Then He said, "My Father is a just king, and there will be no lack in his kingdom." I could not help thinking how wonderful to live in a place like that. All I had ever known was injustice, sorrow and poverty. There was a long pause after this statement, and it seemed to me that He had finished his teaching for the day. Because of my condition and having to keep my distance, I decided to take the opportunity and called out, "Master, have mercy on me, a leper." People turned in horror to stare in my direction, but Jesus looked at me and, with great kindness, pointed His finger at me and said, 'Daughter, be healed of your infirmity. Go show yourself to the priests.'

'Soon after that, Jesus healed my mother as well. It was the most wonderful thing anyone could have done for us. I can't begin to tell you what an impact He has made on our lives. My mother and I rejoice every day for the health and strength He has given us.'

Mary, the mother of Jesus, was sitting at the family table with Joseph of Arimathea and other family members, when suddenly Jesus appeared at her side. Her joy was electric, and she exclaimed in delight, 'Jesus, oh Jesus, how wonderful to see you!'

Then the other members of the family began to exclaim with great joy, 'Jesus, oh Jesus, how wonderful! We were hoping you would come today.'

At the sound of His name, people at other tables turned around to see what was happening, and as they expressed their joy at seeing Him, others did too, and soon there was a chorus of celebration. People began to stream forward towards Him, and He hugged them all and blessed them. His touch was electrifying and seemed to strengthen their resolve to follow Him, no matter what. The whole crowd gathered around him; nobody wanted to be left out.

Peter, first on the scene as always, began to organise the crowd and moved them back to a comfortable distance from Jesus, then told them all to sit down on the lawn so everyone could see and hear everything. Brutus joined the crowd sitting on the lawn. As he sat there and watched Jesus talk to His followers, he hoped that he would have one more opportunity to talk to this extraordinary man who gave of Himself so freely to everyone. He seemed to care for people in a way that set Him apart.

Jesus shifted His gaze and looked out over the heads of the crowd until He spotted Brutus. Their eyes met and held, just as they had on that fateful day not so long ago. They smiled at each other. That smile spoke volumes, and Brutus would always treasure the memory of it. He was grateful for the friendship that had developed between the two of them. He had no idea why Jesus had sought him out the way He did but was very grateful that He had. To see Him again was heartwarming, and he wondered if he would be able to talk to Him later, but with all the crowd gathered around Him, it didn't seem possible.

Every eye was on Jesus and every ear intent on every word He spoke. He certainly had the crowd's full attention, but just then, a little cool breeze made Brutus take stock of his surroundings. He realised that he had been so absorbed in what Jesus was saying that he had not noticed how quickly time had slipped away, and how late it was. He realised that he would have to leave immediately as he would be expected back at the barracks. He was disappointed that he had not had the opportunity to talk to Jesus but knew that he must find Adamas and leave immediately.

Brutus headed off in the direction he had seen the servant take his horse and came across Adamas grazing in a field along with several other horses and some donkeys. He led the big gelding on the rein some distance from the edge of the crowd as quietly as he could, not wanting to disturb or distract anyone. They were nearly at the gates when he heard that familiar voice behind him say, 'Thank you for coming, Brutus.'

Brutus spun around and joy flooded his being, as Jesus continued, 'It's been so good to see you again; I was hoping you would come today. When I saw you in the crowd, I knew that I must talk to you because I will be going back to my Father soon.'

Brutus felt nostalgia at the thought of Jesus's departure and his own imminent return to Rome. He had enjoyed his stay in Jerusalem, the people he had met and new friends he had made, but simply replied, 'I have thought long and hard about all the things we discussed in Capernaum and have decided to become a follower of your teachings. I have come to the realisation that you gave up everything you had and held dear for the sake of humanity. You laid aside your divinity and came to earth as a helpless baby, subject to ordinary people and, in time, grew to be a man with red blood in your veins. You lived your life helping people. Not only that, but as God in the flesh, you were willing to humble yourself to the very ones you had created. And you suffered the cruellest death known to man for the sake of all mankind. You gave everything you had to give, you gave your own body in death, so that people could be brought back into a right relationship with your Father. I don't know of anything more noble than that, and I find you to be a purpose driven and courageous man. How could I not want to be associated with you. I have decided to leave the military and get married on my return to Rome.

'That will be wonderful,' said Jesus with a smile.

'Also, my parents are elderly and would like me to take over the running of our estate, so they will be pleased to hear my news.'

'Keep in touch with my disciples while you are in

Jerusalem. You know they will assist you if you need any help.'

'Yes, I know. A friendship has developed between us. Your disciples are a great group of men, and I feel very comfortable when I am with them.'

The two men embraced warmly. Their relationship was congenial and a far cry from anything Brutus could have imagined. Waving their goodbyes, he cantered away.

BACK AT THE BARRACKS

At the barracks, life continued as usual for Marcus, Lucius and Stephanas, the three soldiers picked to assist Brutus in the execution of Jesus. The seamless robe had been cleaned and was lying across Stephanas's bed. The man who had taken such care with it and painstakingly restored it to its former glory had left it on his bed, knowing that he would pass it on to its rightful owner. The camaraderie among these men was second to none, and he mused that it would be difficult to find a more gallant group of men. The money belt Stephanas had won that day was hanging on a hook on the wall above his bed, along with a host of other war trophies he had collected over the years. He was proud of his achievements in the army and that Brutus had hand-picked him for this assignment; these mementoes gave voice to his achievements. Stephanas was well known for his fastidious attention to detail and his willingness to go the extra mile. These qualities brought him to the attention of the officers, who knew they could rely on him to carry out an order to the last detail.

When Stephanas finally got into bed that night, he was bone weary. A wound to the lower part of his right leg, that he had sustained in battle sometime previously, was a source of constant pain. The wound had healed but had left him with an angry red mark, together with some nerve and tissue damage. Some days were worse than others, and today had been a bad day. He was pleased to be able to get into bed at last and take the weight off his painful leg. Too tired to make the extra effort to take the seamless robe through to Brutus's quarters, he decided to leave it draped over his bed till the morning. When he had rested his aching limbs, he would take the time to pass it on. Stephanas slept soundly. It was the deep sleep of an exhausted man but next morning, at the sound of the bugle, he was the first one up and out of bed and got straight into his daily routine. It was not until late afternoon that he had time to reflect, and he realised his leg had not troubled him all day. *How amazing!* he thought, *This, is the first time in months that I have been free of pain.*

A few days later, Stephanas ran into Amos, the man Brutus had commissioned to wash and restore the seamless robe to its original beauty. The two men got into a conversation about the robe. Amos was clearly anxious and wanted to be assured that the robe had been passed on to Brutus. It occurred to Stephanas that this meeting had been skilfully arranged by Amos, who simply wanted peace of mind. Be that as it may, he was a likeable fellow, and the conversation went from topic to topic until Stephanas found himself listening as Amos explained to him that, since washing the seamless robe, he had been free of arthritic pain in his hands.

'I can believe that,' Stephanas said, 'because since I slept with the robe over my bed, I have been free of the pain I had in my right leg from an old war wound. You realise, of course, that the robe belonged to Jesus of Nazareth.'

'Yes, I knew that,' said Amos. 'He was a powerful speaker with very different ideas from anyone else. They say He did many miracles when He was alive and had a great following. I have heard that He had great compassion for people and healed everyone who came to Him for help. It didn't matter what the problem was; he healed them all.'

For a moment, Amos stopped speaking. His voice became almost a whisper, and the expression on his face showed wonder as he said, 'I hear He called himself the Son of God.'

There was another pause in the conversation, then Amos continued. 'Those poor people had nowhere to go for the help they so desperately needed, and what a difference He made to so many lives. We all thought these people were so unimportant and it didn't matter how we treated them, but to Him nobody was unimportant. Now, this is only for your ears, master Stephanas: He was a good man and what happened to Him should never have happened.'

'Yes,' said Stephanas, 'I realise that now, and I think we all felt the same way. Even Brutus has been to see Him, and we all deeply regret any part we played in His execution. But at the time we had no alternative; we were under orders.'

'What a terrible death for an innocent man,' said Amos. 'Just talking about it gives me a sense of shame and guilt, but they say He has come back from the dead and has been seen by a lot of people. They can't all be wrong.'

'That's right. He was last seen at Joseph of Arimathea's home. Brutus was there that afternoon He was invited by a group of the teacher's disciples, and he said that he counted more than five hundred people in the crowd' (1 Corinthians 15:6).

The conversation seemed to have reached a natural conclusion and both men made their excuses and returned to their respective duties.

The men under Brutus's command were becoming increasingly impatient to go home. Rome and all that was familiar seemed like a million miles away, and they were taking out their frustrations on one another. Marcus was not part of the furore but lay on his bed staring at the ceiling. It was in quiet moments like this away from the others that he felt guilt nagging at his conscience. His mind travelled back to that morning in the courtyard of the Praetorium, and he felt ashamed of the way he had acted. Marcus cringed at the thought of it all as the memories came flooding back to haunt him. He had been the one to thrust his spear into

Jesus's side to make sure He was dead. It had been his idea to roll the dice and gamble for His clothes. The remorse deepened, and he felt the need to clear his head. Maybe a long hot bath would help. He hoped to find people there who were in a better frame of mind. He wanted to be with people who were laughing and joking. With that thought in mind, he put on the tunic that had belonged to Jesus and walked through the barrack room heading for the bath house.

When the men saw him wearing the tunic, they were delighted to find someone or something they could ridicule. As the comments flew back and forth, the barrage that came against Marcus was overwhelming, and even his quick-witted sarcasm was no match for the chorus of male voices.

At this point, Stephanas stepped into the middle of the room and stood beside Marcus. 'You may mock and scoff,' he said, 'but I want to tell you something. From the night I slept with His robe over my bed until now, I have not had any pain in my right leg. And Amos tells me that he has been free of arthritic pain in his hands since he washed the robe for Brutus. You can scoff all you want to, but I am telling you there was something very different about that man.'

By this time, the barrack room had become quiet, and a sober mood had settled over the men. 'Funny you should say all those things,' said Marcus, 'because while you were talking to the men, I got a mental picture of my sister-in-law who is barren but would really love to have some children. So, I have decided to let her use the tunic for a while and see if it changes things for them.'

'I've got the strangest feeling that it will,' said Stephanas, 'because that was this man's nature. He never got tired of helping people and always gave children special attention. He would put them on His knees and bless them.'

As Marcus stepped outside the building and made his way to the bath house, he met Brutus heading in the same direction. After he had greeted him in the customary manner, Brutus said, 'I have some good news. We will be leaving for Rome as soon as a ship can be found that is large enough to carry us and all our equipment. I am not sure at this stage if the men will have to march all the way to the port, or if transport can be arranged, but one thing is sure – we must start preparing for our trip home. I will come and tell the men when I have made the arrangements.'

'That will change the atmosphere in our barrack room,' said Marcus with a cheeky grin. 'The men talk about going home all the time.'

They walked the short distance together, but as they got near the baths, Brutus spotted a tall, lean man in a cavalry officer's uniform and realised that Flavius was just ahead of them. With a slight nod of his head and flick of his eyes, he motioned for Marcus to leave him. Brutus lengthened his stride with ease and caught up with Flavius. They entered the building together and went into a room where they could leave their uniforms and then relax and socialise in the hot water.

Brutus began to tell Flavius of their imminent return to Rome, and how he and his men were looking forward to going home. Then the conversation turned to transportation and the need to find a suitable vessel.

'Your best bet would be to sail from Caesarea,' said Flavius. 'It is a very busy port and only a two-day march from here. I will not be using my wagons for some time, so you can use them if you need to.'

Brutus extended his hand in gratitude as they parted.

The next day, Marcus folded the tunic that had belonged to Jesus and stacked it with other items of his clothing in a neat pile. For one brief moment, the sight of it made him feel ashamed, but as he thought about his brother and sister-in-law, it gave him comfort, and he looked forward to the day they would return to Rome and he could give it to her. He would tell her who it had belonged to, and that His clothes seemed to have healing powers, so that she would be aware and take note of anything out of the ordinary. He hoped that he would soon hear the good news that a baby was on the way. It lifted his spirits to think that he would be helping these two special people fulfil their dreams of having children. If he never saw the tunic again, that would be all right, because it brought back too many painful memories. Besides, if it would help someone else, then he could not ask for a better outcome.

A few days later, Brutus called his men together to give them the good news they had been waiting for. He had managed to arrange their passage back to Rome, and the cavalry officer, Flavius, had kindly offered to lend them some of his wagons. Before he could say any more, loud cheers of jubilation erupted as the men expressed their pleasure and excitement. As soon as Brutus left the room, the men began to pack up their personal belongings ready for the trip home.

Lucius picked up the sandals he had won and studied them. He noticed that one was damaged, and they were scuffed and bloodstained. His mind travelled back over recent events, and he remembered how Jesus had stumbled and fallen on the cobbled street. Could that have been the moment the shoe was damaged? He felt for this man who had suffered so much, and he would have helped Him carry His cross, but that was not the Roman way. He was not allowed to show kindness, or he himself would have been punished. He was relieved to see Brutus pull Simon of Cyrene out of the crowd and make him carry the cross. As he studied the sandals, he realised that some of the blood could be removed, and he wiped it away with a damp cloth. The rest would have to stay, as it had soaked into the soft leather and could not be removed. He tried them on to see if they fitted him and found that they fitted perfectly. They were beautifully made and had very good ankle support. He knew that he could have the tear repaired and, mindful that there seemed to be healing powers in Jesus's clothes, he packed them away carefully.

There was great excitement in the air, for they were going home. And they would not have to carry everything themselves on the long march to the port. If they got tired, they would be able to hitch a ride on the wagons for part of the way. The men were ecstatic at the thought of it all; they had longed for this day, and it had finally arrived.

HOME AT LAST

There was a distinct crisp freshness in the early morning air as the men prepared to disembark from the ship that had brought them home. They stood in line and waited to be given the items they would be required to carry on the long march from the port to the barracks. When all was ready, there was a gruff command from Brutus, and the men lined up ready to advance. On a second command, they marched down the gangplank in unison, a formidable sight to behold. The shopkeepers, who had opened their doors early to be ready for every possible sale, gazed in awe at the spectacular display of might as the men marched past them to the beat of drums. The sound of their marching feet could be heard long after they had disappeared from sight.

As the soldiers came through the main gates of their barracks, everything was suddenly very familiar. They were home at last, hot baths awaited them and plenty of food, and they would be able to sleep on home soil for the foreseeable future. They could relax and finally enjoy these simple pleasures. Tomorrow they would be required to get straight back into combat training and physical fitness exercises.

A Roman soldier had a gruelling lifestyle, for he would have to prepare in the winter months to be ready to go to war in the spring and fight until it was not practical to fight anymore. Rome was constantly at war, ever seeking to conquer people of foreign lands, to have power and dominion over them and to exploit their wealth and natural resources. The soldiers were known to be strong in mind and body but did not have a long life, because they were constantly engaged in hand-to-hand combat and would often succumb to the prevailing diseases of the country they were in.

At last, Brutus was on home soil. With a sense of relief, he began to carry out his plans for his future. There were many issues to be dealt with; not the least of these was to send his servant, Maximus, to his family home with a letter for his parents to let them know of his plans. Maximus would need to bring a wagon back so that he could transport all his personal effects home. His personal possessions had been stored away safely under lock and key while he had been posted overseas.

As Maximus would not be back for some time, he decided to re-familiarise himself with all the items he had kept stored in the beautifully carved wooden chest he had purchased from a local dealer. The chest had been delivered to his quarters and placed in his bedroom. Upon entering the room, he drew the lamp closer to the chest so he could see the contents more clearly. He opened the lock and lifted the lid. He was amazed at the array of beautiful objects all gleaming in the lamp light, things he had forgotten he had. He lifted out one piece at a time so he could examine it more closely, taking in the details and exquisite workmanship of each item, all once much-loved family possessions. The sight of all these items gave him great pleasure, but sadly they had been acquired from looting the bodies of the opposing armies, brave men fighting to preserve what was rightfully theirs, men he had killed on the battlefield. As he took each item from the wooden chest, he could still recall the circumstances, the time and the place where the skirmish had taken place. His life was about to change dramatically. As he handled the items, he became aware of mixed feelings, knowing that the relationships and friendships he had formed, and that were part of his everyday life, would soon be a thing of the past, and that his daily routine would never be the same again. His rank and title had earned him the respect he enjoyed. Doubts began to gnaw at his mind, and he wondered if what he was planning was in fact the right thing to do. Pausing for a moment, he cast his mind back over the events that had brought him to this point in his life, and he realised that it was the only way forward for him. He felt very strongly that these wars would continue on for a long time to come and could still be in progress long after he was in his grave. This was not what he wanted for his life anymore. Since his meeting with the man named Jesus, some how he was not the same person. Something on the inside of him had changed; he did not want to fight or kill people anymore, but instead he felt a great longing for a quiet life in a peaceful setting with his wife, and to relieve his elderly parents of the burden of running the family estate.

Then one day, Brutus's slave, Thomas, came looking for him, to give him the news that Maximus had been seen travelling towards the barracks in a wagon pulled by two horses, and that he had another man with him. Brutus was overjoyed at the news and wondered who the other man could be. He did not have long to wait, because early the next morning Maximus came to his quarters to prepare his breakfast and lay out his uniform as usual. With a big smile on his face, he wasted no time in telling Brutus that he had brought the wagon as he had requested, and that his father, Claudius, had accompanied him to the barracks.

What a great reunion for father and son, who had not seen each other for a long time. The culmination of a deep longing to see his son again, and the fact that he was now home again for good, caused tears of joy to roll down the old man's cheeks. With difficulty, he managed to steady his voice to say, 'When your mother and I read your letter telling us of your desire to leave the military, we were so overjoyed that I just had to come with Maximus and welcome you home.'

Then the day arrived when Brutus would leave all that

was familiar behind. It did not take the four men long to load all his possessions onto the wagon, and with merry hearts they set off for the family estate. It was not long before Brutus asked his father, 'How is my mother?'

'She is not well, and still suffers terribly from that old injury to her foot.'

Then Brutus remembered the day he and his brothers had taken the goats out to graze and they had wandered further and further away from the house. When they had finally realised how late it was, it had taken them a long time to round up the goats and herd them home. Their mother, Eunice, not knowing that they were on their way home, had gone to where she thought they would be to look for them. When she could not find them, she had become concerned for their safety and decided to look in another field. Because she was becoming anxious about the time and aware that she still had to cook the evening meal, she decided to take a short cut through a wooded area and followed a narrow pathway through the trees. She had not been on the path long when suddenly she felt the cruel edges of an animal trap close around her ankle. She knew that the worst thing she could do would be to struggle; that would only make her injury more complex. She stayed as calm as possible and called out for help, hoping that someone would hear her. She called out again and again, but to no avail. This was a lonely place and the little pathway was not used very often. As the afternoon wore on and the shadows lengthened, she began to feel desperate. *Nobody will know where I am*, she thought, and fought to keep panic at bay. She called out again and again for help. Then after what seemed like an eternity, she heard voices and saw what looked like men with a torch walking among the trees. With all her might, she shouted as loudly as she could. They seemed to change direction and walk faster and were heading in her direction. She kept calling out, until suddenly the two men appeared on the path in front of her. Without saying a word between them, they prised open the jaws of the animal trap and freed her leg. She was in a lot of pain and was not able to walk. The trap had caused irreparable damage to her ankle and some of the small bones in her right foot. The two men very kindly helped her to get home.

Now, as Brutus, his father and the others arrived at the homestead, his mother was not at the door to greet them, and Brutus wondered why. His father saw the puzzled expression on his face and explained that she was in a lot of pain and did not walk very much anymore. His father led him through the house to where his mother was resting on a couch. She held out her arms to him in welcome and hugged his neck as he bent forward to embrace her. He could see the years of pain had etched their marks on her face, but nothing was going to dampen her joy at having her son home at last. She clapped her hands, and the servants brought out delicious refreshments on platters, and they ate and drank together. The talking and laughter went on and on, until finally the two men could see that Eunice was falling asleep, so Claudius helped her to bed. He would not let Brutus out of his sight, and they continued their conversation in another room. The bond between father and son was very strong and it was as if Brutus had never been away. But, after a while Claudius said, 'We have been talking for hours. I think it's time to go to bed.'

'Before we turn in,' said Brutus, 'I would like to see my mother one more time.'

He followed his father to their bedroom and, as he watched her lying there, he could see the tension on her face. He felt sad that she had suffered so terribly all those years. Then he had an idea and wondered if the seamless robe that had belonged to Jesus would do for her what it had done for Stephanas. Brutus decided to try out his idea because, after all, what harm could it do? She would either be nice and warm with it on her bed, or she would be healed, and he hoped it would be the latter.

'I have brought her something,' Brutus said to his father, and hurried to his bedroom to get the robe from his wooden chest. When he re-entered their bedroom, his father was still standing and gazing at his mother. This made Brutus realise just how much they loved each other, and he hoped that his marriage would be just like his parents' marriage. His father took the robe from him and gently covered his mother's body with it.

They waited for a moment to see if she would stir, and to make sure she was comfortable before leaving her. As they watched, the expression on her face seemed to relax and she snuggled down into the soft warmth of the garment and seemed to be at ease. As they quietly left the room, the gentle smile on his father's face showed his pleasure and the relief he felt that his darling wife was more comfortable.

'You have brought her the best gift possible,' he said, 'because she really struggles with that old injury and has not slept properly for a long time.'

Brutus decided it was too late to tell his father the story of how the robe had belonged to Jesus and how it had helped Stephanas. That story would be best told when they had plenty of time. 'I have many stories to tell you,' he said, 'but now it's time for bed.'

Next morning, when Claudius woke up, it seemed to be late as though he had overslept. Then he remembered that he and Brutus had gone to bed quite late the night before. He looked across to his wife's side of the bed, but she was not there and he wondered what had happened. When he opened the bedroom door, he could not believe the noise coming from the kitchen. It sounded as though the room was full of people all talking at the same time, some were shouting, and others were laughing. He walked towards the kitchen, expecting to find a riot going on in there but, instead, when he opened the door, he could not believe his eyes. There was his precious Eunice, standing in the middle of the room leaning up against the table, with some of the household staff and slaves standing along one wall of the room. When she saw him in the doorway, she called out in excitement, 'Claudius, look! I can walk and I have no pain.' She began to walk towards him, then she changed direction and walked around the table again and again, trailing her fingers on the tabletop to maintain her balance. This made everyone clap and cheer. *So, this was the noise I heard,* he thought.

'Just give me a moment,' he said. 'I am going to get Brutus. I want him to see this.' He returned a few moments later with Brutus. The two men clapped and cheered with everybody else as they watched her walking around the table. With each step, she grew a little stronger.

'Another lap,' called a cheerful voice from the back of the room. Then Claudius clapped his hands, and everyone dispersed and went back to their duties.

'I was wondering if Mother would be healed,' said Brutus. 'This happened because we covered her with the seamless robe last night. I have seen the same thing happen before. The seamless robe is one of the stories I have not had the time to tell you yet.'

'Well, you must tell me right away,' said the excited Claudius. 'In my wildest dreams, I could never have imagined anything like this happening. Your mother walking after all this time – it's like a dream come true.'

Brutus floundered for a moment, not knowing where to

begin with the story of Jesus and His robe but eventually got going and began at the beginning. There was much to tell. He also told his parents how Stephanas's leg was healed from the old war wound. 'That's why I wondered if Mother would be healed as well.'

'After breakfast, you must both come to my room, and we can spend some time having a look at all the things I have in my chest. I have some very costly pieces in there, and they all come with interesting stories. We could spend days talking about them all.'

After breakfast, the three of them went to his bedroom. The servants had put his chest in front of the window seat so they could sit on the seat and view the contents. Brutus took out one item at a time and talked about each one at length, because he knew that his parents were pleased to have him home and thrilled that they could finally spend some time with him. He reached into the chest and the next item he brought out was a strangely shaped object wrapped in a black cloth decorated with a gold edging.

'That looks interesting,' said Claudius. 'What is it? It looks very expensive.'

'I took this from one of our adversaries and it is my prize piece.'

As he spoke, Brutus unwrapped the long thing, which seemed to wobble in his hands. His parents watched, eager to see what the strange object could be. At last, it was unwrapped, and Brutus held it up into the sunlight to display a strikingly exquisite piece. It was made up of black onyx and gold discs arranged alternately on what looked like a leather strap. The contrasting colours made a bold statement, and his parents moved a little closer so they could get a better look at it.

'What is it?' asked Claudius again, as he reached out to take it from Brutus so that he could examine it more closely.

'I took this bridle and these reins from a rival in the opposing army one day in battle. I can still remember him. He was dressed in black from head to toe, and he rode the most magnificent black stallion I have ever seen. I had just killed a man and turned to look for my next opponent when I saw him galloping straight towards me. I knew that I only had seconds to spare, and I only had one chance. I had to act fast, and I had to be deadly accurate, so with all the strength I could muster, I took aim and threw my spear at him. That day of all days, I prayed that the gods would guide my spear and help me. The horse and rider fell within feet of me. He was obviously wealthy and a high-ranking officer. Just the horse blanket alone showed his wealth: it was black and decorated with a red border, and it had red and gold stitching. His tunic was black with gold braid along the hem line, around the neck and across his chest, and his stallion was the most well-bred animal I have ever seen. He was obviously very proud of his horse to dress him in this costly piece. You will notice that each of the black onyx and gold discs is carved with exactly the same pattern.'

Then Brutus shook out the black cloth he had used to wrap it in, so he could show his parents. 'This was part of his tunic,' he said.

'That looks costly to me,' said Claudius. 'The gold braid is exquisite, and he was dressed in a way that would strike fear into the heart of the bravest opponent. You did an outstanding job in bringing him down. Your commander should be pleased with you.'

'Yes, he is, because, when this man fell, it seemed to send a signal to his troops, and they just turned and fled in terror. The panic was electric and gathered momentum as they ran. I called the three men closest to me to come and guard my loot while I led the charge against them, but the fight was over. Our troops followed after them, and it was the easiest victory we have ever had.'

Brutus became a little weary with having to recall all the events and details of his military career, as each item was lifted out of his chest. He was a man of action and wanted to get on with his life, so he said to his parents, 'Have you seen Diana lately? I would like to visit her if I can.'

His mother was the first to speak and she said, 'We have not seen her for a few months, but when we did talk to her, she said that her husband had died recently.'

He was not surprised to hear that she had married, because he had been away from home for many years. 'I would like to go to see her,' said Brutus. 'Do you know where she lives?'

'After her husband died, she brought the two boys back home, and the three of them are now living with her parents on the estate. She just felt it would be a better for the boys to have a home with the extended family and trusted friends and felt that they would feel more secure in that environment.'

'That sounds like a wise decision, and very much like something she would do.'

That evening, Brutus was home at last in familiar surroundings and in his own bed, but as he lay there in the dark room, he could not fall asleep. Memories of his carefree childhood came flooding back; thoughts of Diana and the things they had done together and the places they had enjoyed visiting filled his mind, as though it had only happened yesterday. The two families were neighbours and only a small stream separated the two estates. He could still remember the large stepping stones across the stream. He was never sure who had put those large stones in place, but they allowed easy access, and the two had used those stepping stones to visit each other regularly. His fondest memory of her was seeing her running through the fields with her long dark hair being tossed about by the breeze. She had clear, laughing eyes and a big smile. Unbeknown to her, her strong vivacious personality had sustained him on countless occasions throughout his career, and she had always had a special place in his heart. But his desire to pursue a military career had been strong and one he had not been able to resist. Now that he was home again, he wanted to pick up where he had left off. He was secretly pleased that Diana's husband had died recently, because that left her free, and if there were any other admirers, it would not matter because there had always been something special between them.

The next morning, he rose early to get ready for his big day. There had been one last thing to do before leaving Jerusalem, and that was to buy Diana a present. He had decided to send Maximus out to find perfume makers, with strict instructions to bring back good quality spikenard and make sure it was in a very attractive glass jar. There was also plenty to choose from in his wooden chest. He opened it and went through the items and wondered which of the trinkets she would like the best. Then he saw a lovely pair of dangle earrings made from semi-precious carnelian. They were pear-shaped with a little gold hook at the narrow end, and the beautifully blended shades of honey, peach and apricot brown formed the lower part of the earrings. He felt that they would look stunning against her dark hair, and he hoped that she still wore it long the way she used to. He wrapped the earrings in a pretty piece of silk and tied the loose ends with a matching ribbon.

That done, he set off to visit his childhood sweetheart. He knew the roads well and noticed that nothing had changed much in all the years he had been away. It was a beautiful morning, clear and sunny with a light breeze. It would be a good day to surprise her, he thought impishly, remembering her ready smile and the way she used to laugh at his jokes.

As he drew near the house, he dismounted and, walking beside his horse, he led her to walk on the grass so she would make as little noise as possible. As they entered the tree-lined avenue leading up to the house, he was grateful for the shade and cover of the trees. As they neared the house, he suddenly saw Diana, framed by an archway, standing in the shade of the portico at the front of the house. She looked as lovely as ever; the years had not stolen her beauty. He was pleased to see that her hair, though a shade lighter, was still long, the way she had always worn it.

Should he surprise her as he had planned, or should he simply call out her name? He was aware of the old tenderness he had always felt for her touch his heart again. Then because he could not decide how to approach her, he just stood in the shade of the trees and watched her.

After a while, she must have felt his eyes on her and turned to see who could be watching her. She looked in his direction, until she finally spotted him standing among the trees. 'Brutus, is that you?' she exclaimed with pleasure, her heart beating a little faster and her face lighting up with a smile.

'Yes,' he said. 'It's me. I have left the military, and I am home for good.'

When she heard those words, 'home for good', she could hardly believe her ears. She came out to greet him as he tied his horse to one of the trees. There was grazing for her, and she would be in the shade. That done, he turned to face Diana, and they embraced each other warmly.

The years seemed to melt away, until finally she said to him, 'Let's go inside and see my parents. They often talk about you and will be thrilled to see you again after all these years.'

'Before we do that, I have something for you,' he said and opened a small leather bag hanging from his saddle. He handed her the gifts he had brought for her. As she took them, her smile left him in no doubt of her feelings. They walked indoors, and Brutus was slightly overwhelmed by the warmth and friendliness the family showed as they greeted him. Later, as they sat chatting in the cool shade of the atrium enjoying some tasty refreshments, Diana began to unwrap her gifts. She opened the package containing the jar of spikenard first. 'Oh, Brutus,' she exclaimed with pleasure. 'Spikenard, it's my favourite fragrance, and it's in such a beautiful jar.' Then placing the jar carefully on a table, she untied the little package containing the earrings. 'These are lovely,' she said, as she held them up so the light would show their multicolours. 'I shall enjoy wearing these.'

Brutus felt that he was in his rightful place and truly home. The two families had always been good friends, and he knew that Diana's parents would gladly welcome him into their family.

One day, Brutus and Diana were strolling around the local

market. Some of the stalls were out in the open while others were under cover. They were enjoying the simple pleasures of the moment, and the sights and sounds of people jostling each other for the best bargain. The smell of freshly cooked food and nuts being roasted on the coals hung in the air and made them feel hungry. Just then, a saucy young man with a wide grin stepped out in front of Brutus and held up a small bag.

'Warm nuts for the lady, mister?' he said.

Brutus muttered something under his breath but took the nuts and tossed a small coin at the boy. They walked on, mingling with the crowd and were impressed by the large number of stalls and the great variety of items available for sale. Then out of the corner of his eye, Brutus caught sight of the all-too-familiar uniform of a Roman centurion coming towards them. Who should it be but his old colleague, Titus, who had stepped into his shoes and taken over the command of his soldiers.

Brutus pointed him out to Diana. 'I don't think he has seen us yet,' he said. They turned their backs to the road and allowed him to pass them by, before Brutus turned and tapped him on the shoulder. Titus swung around with his hand on his dagger, ready for anything.

'Brutus!' he exclaimed. 'You old dog, what are you doing here, and who is this beautiful lady?'

'This is Diana, my betrothed.'

'I have a little time to spare,' said Titus. 'I want to know all about the two of you.'

'And I want you to give me news of my men.'

'They are not your men anymore; they are my men.'

They found a trader who sold food and homemade wine. 'The food smells delicious,' said Brutus, and they sat down to enjoy some time together.

After Brutus had been talking for a while, he felt that it was time to switch roles with Titus because he wanted to know how his men had settled down under the new leadership, and how their training was going. He knew that once he got Titus talking, it would be hard to stop him. He was a chatty type of person who loved to tell stories, and if one could get him on a subject, he would expound on the topic in great detail. To get him started, Brutus mentioned the names of Marcus, Stephanas and Lucius, the three he had relied on the most. Titus picked up on Lucius immediately.

'That Lucius,' he said, 'has the most amazing ability to outmanoeuvre his opponents. Last time we had a mock training session of three against one, he mock killed all three opponents in quick succession. It was his quick footwork and the strength in his arms that carried him to safety. I was keen to learn more about his footwork and the way he moved, so I could incorporate it into the training program. But he told me this strange story about the sandals he was wearing. Apparently, they had belonged to the man named Jesus whom the unit had crucified. They looked like ordinary sandals to me; the only difference was that they were bloodstained, but that could hardly make any difference. He said that his sandals were worn out and he needed some new ones. These were the only ones available, so he put them on, and he noticed a change in himself immediately. He said that he was suddenly light on his feet and could manoeuvre his body in such a way that his opponents became confused, and he was able to get the better of them. On top of all that, he found that he was able to walk for miles and not get tired. I must admit that I didn't understand it all, but he certainly had an edge on his opponents.'

'I can understand that story perfectly,' said Brutus, and he told Titus the story of how the old war wound on Stephanas's leg had been healed and how, after Amos had washed the seamless robe, he had lost all arthritic pain in his hands. 'And I am thrilled to tell you about my mother. You see, many years ago, she caught her foot in an animal snare and ever since then had difficulty in walking, because all those little bones in that area of the foot never really healed properly. But the other night, my father and I covered her with the seamless robe that had belonged to Jesus of Nazareth, and in the morning, she was completely healed. We don't know how it happened; we just know that she could walk again. It was a miracle.'

Titus looked at Brutus and noted the earnest expression on his face and the conviction in his tone. He nodded his head, accepting what he had just heard and simply said, 'I must be on my way. We have been talking for hours, and I must finish my shopping and get back to barracks, but it is good to see you both so happy.'

After Titus had left them, Brutus and Diana lingered a little while longer at their table, just enjoying each other's company. Brutus could not remember a time when he had felt so relaxed, and realised that he had made the right decision to leave the military. Being responsible for the training and welfare of all his men was not an easy task. But all that was behind him now, and he was looking forward to a new way of life.

www.ingramcontent.com/pod-product-compliance
Lightning Source LLC
Chambersburg PA
CBHW051710180726
48283CB00004B/1279